BREATHE: EVERYONE HAS TO DO IT

BREATHE: EVERYONE HAS TO DO IT

Christopher Fowler

First published in England in 2004 by

Telos Publishing Ltd
61 Elgar Avenue, Tolworth, Surrey, KT5 9JP, England
www.telos.co.uk

Telos Publishing Ltd values feedback. Please e-mail us with any
comments you may have about this book to:
feedback@telos.co.uk

ISBN: 1-903889-67-7 (paperback)
Breathe © 2004 Christopher Fowler.

ISBN: 1-903889-68-5 (hardback)
Breathe © 2004 Christopher Fowler.

Printed in India

1 2 3 4 5 6 7 8 9 10 11 12 13 14 15

British Library Cataloguing in Publication Data.
A catalogue record for this book is available from the British
Library.

1. WELCOME TO SYMAXCORP

Welcome to the bad world of big business. Companies are like icebergs, mostly hidden from view. Or they're like hives, where everyone is given a specific job and a limited amount of knowledge. Almost any analogy works, because commerce is amorphous and elusive. If the events of this story have already happened, you won't be told about them. You'll be suspicious from the outset, of course. You know how these things tend to shape up. The evil bosses, the downtrodden workers, yadda, yadda.

But this particular company started life as a place that would benefit everyone. It was all planned out by a decent man, albeit a man with little understanding of people and how they work.

It began as an architectural model, a tower of smooth, white-painted balsa and plastic, surrounded by neat round trees. At its base strolled tiny plastic couples. The nearby river was a sheet of shiny blue perspex. The effect was one of space and light, a monument to human endeavour.

The reality is a glittering black jewel box, a saturnine, crystalline spear called the SymaxCorp building. As impersonal as only a modern building can be. The walkways around its rain-bleached base now resemble electronic circuitry, paths snaking between terminals, sparking trade into life. No couples stroll here by the scudding brown river. Workers come, do the job and get the hell out. How can you be comfortable in a building where the windows don't open? Where the walls reflect back your own lonely image?

Did the designers and architects believe their own lies? Did they ever think, as they peered into the model, that this glass prison would offer freedom and happiness?

It is nearly midnight, and everyone has gone home now. Out of hours, the area has as much life as the surface of the moon.

The entire business district is built in a crescent around the bend in the river. It is less than five years old, but some of the trees have been planted fully grown to provide instant ambience. There are no homes or shops, or old men walking dogs. There is only the fierce crackle of commerce between the hours of nine and six. SymaxCorp is the latest building to be completed, a monolithic cathedral of industry designed not for the benefit of the individual, but for the unification of the masses. Although it is the personification of order, it has not been constructed on a human scale. Everything about it dwarfs the experience of living. If Albert Speer had lived on, this is what he'd have built.

Up on the twentieth floor, a single light shines bright. A salaryman called Felix Draycott is still working, sweating in the icy air, grabbing the last pages of his document as they leave the printer. He hates running out hard copies, but Clarke, his supervisor, refuses to read electronic documents. He hurries between the deserted workstations, heading for the row of glass boxes – individual offices granted only to supervisors – where Clarke stands waiting.

Clarke's office is decorated with trophies for sporting events – rugby, football, swimming – and endless pictures of his son, in muddy, bloody kit, gap-toothed and downcast, the reluctant champion. There are cups and plaques, and a mounted cricket bat presented by minor royalty. The supervisor is living, through his son, the athletic career that he could never have had himself. Pathetic, really.

Clarke is overweight, red and balding, with a scary combover and a shiny leather built-up boot to compensate for a short leg, which he thinks no-one notices. He's fifty-three years old, stout and surprisingly strong. And on the inside? Well, let's just say that he's been very angry about his life for a very long time.

He reads the document, pacing around the seated Felix.

'Drains. Drainage. Dampers? ... Ducts. Disposal, waste.'

Felix waits for more.

'See under Suction.' Clarke flips back a few pages. Felix waits with sweating palms cupped between his thighs.

'Binary. Bins. Bin liners. Bin fires, small.' He turns the page. 'Computers. Coronaries. Cardiac arrest. Very impressive. You've really done your homework, Draycott.' He riffles to the end of the document, reading the conclusion. 'I like a man who makes up his mind about something.'

'I talked to the R&D people, ran simulations, drew my own conclusions,' Felix ventures. 'Obviously it's not what you want to hear ...'

'No, it's a remarkable piece of work.' There's a *but* coming. Felix holds his breath.

'But it's a pity you've made so many spelling errors. Small slips, but so important, I feel. "i before e except after c". Here. Here. Here. *Here*. It's not hard to remember. And what's this, biro?' Clarke jabs at the page with a fat finger. Even in the freezing machine-fed air, Felix can feel the sweat dripping down his back.

Clarke puts down the document and casually removes the cricket bat from its chromium mount. 'Tell me, do you ever play cricket?'

'No,' Felix admits. 'Football, sometimes.' He is suddenly aware of his proximity to Clarke's built-up boot. 'That is, uh ...'

Clarke takes a practice swing that comes perilously close to Felix's face. He's glancing back down at the document. 'This is a problem for the board. But I think I can crack it.'

'That's a weight off my mind,' Felix admits. He wasn't too sure how Clarke would react.

Clarke suddenly swings the bat down hard, cracking Felix a shattering blow over the skull, laying him out across his now-exploded chair. The top of Felix's head is as flat as a deflated football. Blood is leaking from his ears.

'I'm a tolerant man,' Clarke tells him, not that Felix can hear, 'but there's no excuse for poor spelling.' He drags Felix's body off by the collar, down the darkened corridors, humming happily to himself.

The window through which Clarke can be seen is one of thousands, and now the light is extinguished. Endless windows, millions of workspaces. The black mirrored buildings rise up, vast, dark, dense, muscular with struts and cables, soaring floor by floor, until they blot out the sky.

2. MONDAY

The same deserted business district of the city is still silent at dawn. Then a single road-sweeper turns into the street. Window-cleaners set to work. Office cleaners appear beyond the windows, pushing vacuum cleaners across floors. Fluorescent lights flicker on. The pistons of business slowly rise and fall. The great engine of the city is coming to life.

Now an astonishing mass of commuters pours from trains and buses, over bridges, across roads, densely packed and determined, a civilian army on the march. People in stations, at bus stops, weaving between each other as more and more arrive. Yawns, coffee-cups, rubbed faces, snatched cigarettes. Workers through train windows, alighting on platforms, heading to work in their thousands. The crystal citadels unlock their doors as employees filter in.

It is the height of the rush hour. Through the commuter crowds on the platform, a young man called Ben Harper makes his way to work. He smooths his sticky-up hair, too alive to his surroundings to be a typical member of the workforce, too open and innocent and obvious. It's his first day, but you can tell that just by looking at him.

Ben's suit is too new. His shoes are too shiny. He grimaces and pulls a pin out of his shirt collar, then peels a price sticker off his briefcase. The shoes hurt because he's used to trainers. He has never worn a tie before in his life. It took him twenty minutes to do the damned thing up.

Ben stands looking at the awesome SymaxCorp building. *My new home*, he thinks proudly. The windows glitter darkly in the early sunlight. This is where Ben has come to begin his corporate existence. He nervously checks his clothes and his minty breath, keen to make a good first impression. After looking up anxiously at the tower, he screws up courage and walks to the great doors, the Scarecrow entering Oz.

Crossing the gleaming, black marble lobby floor is an act of courage in itself. The entrance is vaulted and vast, shafted with angles of light, modern gothic, Sir Christopher Wren crossed with Tim Burton.

Behind him, a uniformed janitor follows with an electric cleaner, wiping away Ben's footprints as quickly as he leaves them. The building's impersonal atmosphere is already at work on him. It does that to people – you don't even notice it's happening until you've changed.

Ben feels out of place, bogus, an interloper here under false pretences. His collar feels as if it's choking him. He coughs, asks at the desk where he should go, and is directed to the elevators.

He manages to enter one of the daunting steel lifts, but has trouble getting the doors to shut. The buttons won't respond to his touch. He has had little experience of technology. Just before the doors close, a girl steps in. She wears the corporate armour of high finance, black slacks and a black top. A gold neck-chain. Cropped blonde hair with muted highlights. Pretty, in an unattainable way. Ben reaches across her and tries the doors again, but nothing happens.

'Here.' The girl reaches down and removes her shoe, then smacks the destination panel with it. 'It always does this.' The elevator jerks and starts up. 'Technology. Just 'cause it looks good, doesn't mean it'll do what you tell it to do.' She smiles absently at him, then stares ahead.

Ben stands uncomfortably beside her as they wait for their floor. He goes to speak, then changes his mind.

The lift stops and the doors open. The futuristic reception area of SymaxCorp beckons. Black smoked glass, polished steel, underlighters; a cross between a Fred and Ginger dance set and a Mayfair car showroom. Flat-screen monitors display the caring side of the sharing corporation; waterfalls, rainforests, sunsets, horribly soothing music that sounds like an Enya rip-off.

Ben approaches the receptionist, a tousle-haired and frazzled-looking woman with visible bra-straps. She's wearing a name badge: THOMPSON. She can barely be seen over her desk, which is finished in grey granite. He listens as she complains on the phone to someone, half-heartedly trying not to be overheard.

'Right across the top of my head, like a red-hot knife sawing into my brain, back and forth, back and forth, back and forth. And then I bring everything up.'

Ben coughs. 'Excuse me?'

Ms Thompson covers the phone as if caught selling state secrets. 'Can I help you?'

'Ben Harper. I'm starting work here today?'

The receptionist replaces the phone and does something extraordinary. She drops her head hard onto the counter.

Ben is understandably alarmed. 'Are you all right?'

'It's nothing,' she mumbles. 'Just a headache. You're expected. Please take a seat.' She keeps her head down as he walks away.

Ben seats himself on a huge, squeaky leather sofa.

'NOT THERE!'

Ben jumps up in alarm.

'That one's got – something wrong – with it,' the receptionist explains.

He studies the skinny identikit corporate drones passing through the reception area and realises that, outwardly at least, he has nothing in common with them. He watches the video monitors. The thoughtful transatlantic voiceover intones good things about SymaxCorp – something about 'The Environment You Deserve', and, 'Wouldn't it be good if everything was this easy?'.

After five minutes he is collected by another name-tag. This one reads: FITCH. No first name. It belongs to a thick-waisted, thick-ankled, efficient young woman with dry ginger hair and an intimidating manner. Ben rises and goes to shake her hand, but she just clips a clearance card on his lapel. She does it with a little gun, and he has a feeling that the card won't be removable.

'Glad to have you on board, Mr Harper. This contains a chip with your security clearance. Code 7.'

'Is that good?'

'Codes start at 100 and go all the way down to zero. You get the idea.'

Ben nods. 'I think I do.'

'It means there are six levels below you, but they're …'

'Primates?'

'Not far off.' She points to his badge. 'You're required to wear it at all times on the premises. Try not to drop it down the toilet, as replacement cards will be docked from your salary. Come with me.'

'Please, call me Ben.'

'We don't use first names here, Mr Harper. I don't favour the personal touch.'

'Nice.'

'It's not meant to be cosy, I'm not your mother. Your OOC is me, then Mr Clarke.'

'OOC?'

'Order Of Command. You are familiar with corporate terminology. The supervisors prefer electronic exchange over face-time.'

'We'll probably all get to be pals over a fag break,' says Ben, then bites his tongue.

'This building does not have a cancer verandah. Smoking is a dismissable offence. Think of this as a military operation.'

'Do we get uniforms?'

'You're already wearing it. Remember, all commerce is war.'

'You issue firearms as well?'

'I so wish.' She hands Ben a DVD in a steel slipcase embossed with the word SYMAXCORP. 'Think of this as a holy bible with stiffer penalties for rule-breaking. Please run it and memorise the key points. You may be required by law to answer a questionnaire.' She stacks hard copy documents into his arms. 'You'll also need to read these. As Health and Safety Officer, you may talk to staff only about health and safety issues directly affecting your department. Your first report will be due this Friday.'

Ben tries a tentative smile. It usually works. 'Well, I'm happy,' he tells her.

'Don't waste a smile on me, Mr Harper, you won't be the son I never had.' Fitch turns on her chunky heel and stalks away.

Ben looks around. The offices are dark, silver-grey slate and cherrywood, the new colours of corporate cool. The work-floor is futuristic, ergonomic, designed to prevent time-wasting, a mix of odd perspectives that sometimes curve unexpectedly around corners. There's even a burbling fountain surrounded by grey pebbles and Japanese plants. Fierce little spots of light pinpoint the workstations like static prison searchlights. It's elegant but weirdly oppressive. Touches of humanity exist in the way staff have decorated their booths; a photo pinned here, a small vase of flowers there. The workstations still look like hutches. The semi-private supervisor offices line the open centre, underlit glass boxes that are uncomfortably reminiscent of cages for battery hens.

The staff are highly focused. Workers flit quickly and efficiently or remain hunched at workstations like gargoyles, concentrating on their net-linked computer screens. Ben is perversely excited by the energy and technology he sees all around him. He sees ergonomic headsets and lower back pain, call-waiting and eye strain. He'll have a lot to do.

He examines his workstation, checking the drawers, and is surprised to find that the bottom one has not been cleared out. There are odd items in this little haven of untidiness; photobooth strips, a conker on a string, an uncleaned mug, a pair of socks, yards of tinfoil, a fierce-looking army knife, lots of aspirin bubblepacks.

Ben doesn't see that he has been seated next to the girl from the elevator. The name on her tag reads: JAMESON. She doesn't appear to have noticed him, or perhaps she's just too busy. Needing to load the DVD, Ben surreptitiously attempts to turn on his computer, but can't find the right button. He climbs around the

15

back of his desk, searching for it.

The girl's noticed him now, and watches in amusement as he tries to discover how to turn the iMac on. After letting him fumble about for a while, she leans over and discreetly boots the computer up for him.

'Bottom left,' she whispers, and points.

Ben feels for the button but still can't find it.

'No, your other left. You've never used one of these before, have you?'

Ben feigns indignance. 'Of course I have. I'm just used to a different type. Uh, brand. You know, model.'

She smiles witchily. 'You use firewire or infrared for Powerpoint spreadsheets and Word docs?'

'Oh, well,' he says casually, 'you know, either really. Both. Whatever, I don't mind.'

'Which OS did you train on, then? Ten?'

He studies the ceiling, thinking. 'Oh, er, the usual one. Yeah, ten, probably, or maybe eleven.'

'Okay, sport, it's all yours. Take it away. Let's see what you can do.'

Ben is screwed. Aware of being watched, he tentatively taps the keyboard and shuts everything down again. The girl scoots her chair beside his and holds out her hand.

'I'm Miranda, corporate slut.'

'You don't look –'

'Corporate, I know. What I mean is, I'm a temp. That's how they see us, the management. High pay, low dignity. And you don't know your way around an iMac. We met in the lift.'

'The shoe hammerer.'

'Don't worry, I'm gentler than I look. Listen, I'll keep your secret. Just tell me what the hell you think you're doing here.' Ben gives her a look of bruised innocence. 'Oh, come on. Anyone can see you're a company virgin. How did you ever get this gig? Is your daddy a director? Can't be your mummy, this place has a glass ceiling. I've worked everywhere, they're all the same.'

Ben thinks for a moment and mumbles. 'I – uh – well ...'

Miranda mirrors his innocent look and returns it bigger. Maybe he should level with her.

'Shit. Well, the truth is, a friend helped me make up my CV.' He pulls a disc from his pocket. Miranda takes it from him and inserts it into the iMac. She opens the only file and examines his CV on screen. Apparently he has worked at three of the hottest companies in the city. Yeah, right.

'Pretty fucking unconvincing. And you got away with this?'

Ben checks his watch and pleads with Miranda. 'For just over three minutes. Look ...'

'Miranda. Like in *The Tempest*.'

'Miranda, I need this job,' he pleads. Other workers have noticed their conversation and are pretending, rather obviously, not to listen.

'But you've never done anything like it before.'

'No. I was a hospital carer.'

Miranda scrolls down through the document and finds a second CV – this must be the real one, because it's a lot less impressive. It runs to all of three lines. 'Bit of a career jump, wouldn't you say?' She reads on. REASON FOR TERMINATION. 'Jesus, kicked out for organising a strike. Why do you even keep a copy of this?'

'To remind me,' he explains.

'I wouldn't, not around here. The central server searches everyone's hard drives. Erase it if you're planning to stay.'

'I have to make this work.' He doesn't want to beg, but he will if necessary. 'I can do it. It's Health and Safety, how hard can it be?'.

'Harder than you think. But I may be able to help you. '

Miss Fitch walks past. Her X-ray glare causes Miranda to break off. She waits for the all-clear before resuming.

'We're not supposed to be talking.' She points to the tiny CCTV camera in the corner above their workstations. 'It's activated every time anyone moves their chair. It picks up signs of fraternisation and relays them to the management monitors. You should keep a screensaver made from a worksheet so that you can default to it when a supervisor passes. And put a pair of sunglasses on your desk. You can see who's prowling around behind you.'

'How do you know this stuff?' he asks. Maybe she's older than she looks.

'I'm a temp on 100WPM/1BB. We know everything.' She waves the question aside as she ejects his disc and slips it back in the case. 'Hundred words a minute and one bathroom break a day. Highest rating. I don't have to work here.'

'Then why do you?'

'They pay more. I'll go with anyone. In a strictly business sense.' A quick smile. Miranda's voice carries, and others start to notice when she's not getting on with her work. Ben means to look busy and committed, but it's not easy.

'But why is this place –'

'No more questions. Seal those luscious lips.' She holds a finger to her mouth. 'I'll meet you at the refreshment station in half an hour.'

They stand before the coffee machine like spies exchanging secrets. Miranda points to another CCTV camera above them as she spoons in Nescafé. 'The supervisors time our breaks. We're not allowed tea because we're sponsored by a coffee company.'

'What about mineral water?'

'Coca Cola. Approved company brands only. So why would you want to work here?'

'The money, and I've got a lousy employment history. After the strike, I had a kind of a breakdown. I'm not good in stressful situations.'

She hands him a styrofoam cup. 'Well, you really picked the wrong place this time.'

'Look, I just need to make some cash. Toe the line, be like everyone else and keep my mouth shut.'

'You don't look like someone who can do that.' She's flirting with him. She couldn't be, could she?

'I can do it,' he says unconvincingly. 'I'll fit in and earn some hard cash if it kills me.'

'It might do.' She sips coffee with a smile. 'The last guy who

18

had your desk disappeared.'

Ben reads his on-screen manual. Under DUTIES it has: ASCERTAIN WELFARE OF ALL STAFF IN YOUR RESPONSIBILITY AREA AND FILE WEEKLY REPORT TO HEAD SUPERVISOR. Thirty pages of small print follow the heading, but he skips that part.

'Okay.' Broadly speaking, it sounds easy enough. Ben one-finger types: ACCESS WELFARE REPORTS FOR:

He highlights all the twentieth floor group members. The screen reads: ACCESS DENIED PERMISSION BY GROUP HEAD: MR CLARKE.

It makes no sense. How can he do his job? There's one way to find out. Ben knocks on the glass wall of Fitch's booth and enters. Fitch is busy and barely bothers to look up.

'I'm unable to access the staff's previous welfare reports, Miss Fitch.'

'You don't need to. You're going to file new ones.' She's marking work, ticking and crossing out, a teacher destroying the lives of her pupils with the flick of a pen. No family pictures here, no knick-knacks, just paperwork, files, signs of a monastic existence.

'How can I do that if I can't see their past complaints?'

'Their past complaints have been dealt with.' Tick. Cross. Cross.

'How do I know that?'

Now she looks up. 'Because I'm telling you.'

'I need to see their personal histories. Can you grant me access?'

'You ask a lot of questions.'

'I'm not getting many answers.'

'Then you'll have to come up with some of your own. Your predecessor was very opinionated, Mr Harper.'

'You make it sound like a bad thing.'

'It was for him. Opinions are valid only if someone wants them.'

Don't rise to it, he tells himself, and leaves. Not a great start. He has to learn to control his mouth.

Ben walks over to Miranda's workstation. 'Is there any reason why I wouldn't be able to access any health reports?'

'After Felix disappeared, Clarke rerouted everything.' Miranda points to the man in the photo-frame on Ben's desk, leans forward and whispers. 'His name was Felix Draycott. He vanished three weeks ago. Worked late one night, failed to turn up the next morning. Didn't even come back to empty his desk. We were told stress.'

'What happened to him?'

'You tell me. You're Health and Safety.' She curls a finger between his shirt buttons, drawing him closer. 'Oh, but there's something else. Something really weird.'

'Miranda, it's my first day.' He removes her hand, although he likes the touch.

'I could make it your last.'

'Please don't do this.'

'Come on, Ben, it's your job to listen and make a report.' She opens her desk and takes out an expensive man's watch. 'His watch was still in his desk. He took it off while he was working because he said his computer affected it. What kind of man would leave a job without taking his Rolex with him? And that's not all –' But Miss Fitch is passing with sheaves of paperwork, a one-woman hardcopy industry. 'Meet us for lunch later. That's all I ask.'

'Us?' asks Ben. 'Who's *us*?'

The dining room is as far from a canteen as Ben can imagine – a brushed steel kitchen galley with modular cream resin seats, a seventies-influenced lunch area set in a tall tropical plant-filled atrium. Even the flowers smell real. The food, too, is fashionably seventies; *coq au vin*, chicken *chasseur*, trout with almonds. Miranda takes Ben to a table. As she does so, she points out another staff member, a balding thirty-year-old with a fussy attitude who's talking earnestly to Fitch.

'Who's that?'

'Mr Swan. He's Fitch's bitch, company spy. If you complain about anything, he'll spout the rules and offer you anger-management courses. I'm on his shitlist; there's a surprise. Fitch is a secret drinker. Eats breath-strips to cover it up but forgets to throw away the empties. She has no life. You can imagine. All the men around here are going bald. Weak sperm or something. Comes from sitting too close to the monitors.'

Mr Clarke clumps past. Ben can't help but notice that he has one leg shorter than the other. The boot tends to draw attention to itself.

'That has to be Mr Clarke. He was supposed to be at my interview, but I think he was off sick.'

'He's the one to be scared of. The head of the department, Felix's old boss. He was the last one to see Felix. Don't stare at the boot.' She waves. 'Hey, Meera, June.'

'Hey, Miranda.' Meera Mangeshkar is a harassed-looking Indian staff member clad in a garish sari, and armed with stacks of zip-drives. June is a heavy-set Caribbean woman with a kind face that naturally reposes in a smile. They join them at the lunch table and shake Ben's hand in turn.

'This is Ben. He's Felix's replacement.'

'Oh, wow.' They give him weird, knowing looks.

'Nice to meet you, Ben,' says Meera politely.

'Meera is our IT genius,' Miranda tells him. 'She's been penalised for breaking the dress code.'

'If you get ten points against you, you're suspended,' Meera explains. 'I'm up to nine.'

'You sound quite proud of it,' says Ben.

'I'm here to make the machines look good. Apart from that, I'm invisible. So I don't wear the kind of regulation IT clothes they expect you to wear, and then I'm not invisible.'

'Nice thinking.'

'Nice tie.' Meera flicks his Tootal with a grin. 'This is June Ayson. She was suspended.'

'For being over office target weight.' June pinches an inch

through her sweater. 'I've got a month left to lose fifteen pounds.'

Ben is appalled. 'You're telling me they have a weight limit here?'

'Well, they can't have a colour bar, and they had to think of something.' June doesn't seem too concerned. She smiles, even, white teeth like peppermint pellets. Perhaps she's crazy. Perhaps they're all crazy.

'Am I right in thinking you're all in trouble with the management?' asks Ben. The group's silence answers his question.

'Oh, well, that's just *great*.'

'Listen to me, Ben,' says Miranda. 'I know you want to keep your nose clean, but we need your help. There's something very fucking weird going on here. It's the building.'

'Yeah,' June agrees, 'it has bad vibrations. Strange stuff happens all the time.'

Ben is deeply unconvinced. 'Like what? Poor feng shui? You've even got a *fountain*.'

'It makes you want to wee all the time,' says June.

'Okay, but you've got everything you could want here.'

Miranda has her cynical face on again. 'Yeah, maybe too much. Ask any of the staff. They all have problems. Everyone talked to Felix because he was Health and Safety. He made a report of his findings. He delivered it, and then he disappeared.'

'I don't see how I can –'

Miranda sighs, like he's missing the point. 'Clarke had a copy of Felix's report. He was supposed to present it to Dracula.'

'Wait, there are vampires now?'

'Dr Hugo Samphire. Chief bloodsucker, the Chairman of SymaxCorp. I searched Clarke's office one night, but I couldn't find it. Maybe you'll have more luck.'

Ben raises his hands in protest. He feels like he's waded out into a river, only to feel the current tugging him away. 'Whoa, whoa, back up! Search his office? If I cause any trouble, they'll kick me out.'

'Only if they find out the truth about you.' Miranda smiles sweetly.

Ben feels himself losing his temper. 'Are you trying to blackmail me? This is my first day, for Christ's sake.'

Miranda leans close and threatening, taps him on the wrist with her dessert spoon. 'Listen pal, before Felix's computer was cleaned out, Meera tried to burn a disk of his files, but his system refused to make a copy, and flagged up the request to Clarke.'

Ben looks from one face to the next. 'This is a joke, right?'

'Don't look at me,' warns Meera, 'I can't even be seen talking to you. I'm on my last point.'

'You could try wearing a skirt,' Ben tells her. 'I bet you've never even been to India. Why look for trouble?'

'Jesus, it's not like I'm asking you to commit a crime, Ben.' Miranda throws the spoon down.

Ben is totally irritated by her attitude. She acts like she owns the place. 'You told Felix something "weird" was going on, and now you think he was, like, silenced or something, and you don't even know what he found out!'

'Oh, we know what he found out.'

'Well, what? Tell me!'

She looks at the others in a moment of silence. 'Why don't I show you?'

Miranda leads Ben across the open-plan office. You can hear the wind whistling around the corners of the building up here. They're level with other workers in other buildings. It's like looking into the other train when you're waiting in a station. 'This is as good a place as any to start.'

A crowd has gathered around one of the water coolers. Inside the plastic water tank, liquid is spinning in a wild whirlpool. 'It happens the same time every day. You can set your watch by it.'

'Electro-magnetic interference,' Meera informs him with a nudge. 'There's too much in here. The more equipment we turn on, the weirder it gets.'

'Show him the pigeons,' suggests June.

Meera takes Ben to the corner of the floor, and points out through the great windows. There are dozens of dead pigeons lining the window ledges, lying on their backs with their feet in the air. Some have been cannibalised. They're missing legs and eyes.

Ben presses his face against the cool glass. 'Mass suicide?'

'They get within a certain radius and keel over.'

'Oh come on, Meera. You're talking about some form of radiation?'

'If it can kill a bunch of birds, what's it doing to our brains? Computers are shielded, they shouldn't cross-resonate, but what if the specs are wrong?'

'I thought they had experts to check this kind of stuff.'

'Yeah, that's me. But equipment's more complicated now. You're living in a world where a pen comes with pages of instructions in a dozen languages. Even your after-shave has a web site. It doesn't mean that anyone knows what they're doing.' Meera looks around to make sure the CCTV cameras can't see them, then removes a panel from the wall. Inside, thousands of tiny red insects scurry over the cables. 'Know what these are?'

Ben has never seen anything like it. They swarm onto the floor, miniscule creatures buzzing over and around his shoes. He takes a step backwards.

'Computer mites. Every building in the city has them. Just not this many. Pest controllers came in and sprayed, but they were back the next week, bigger and stronger.'

'Maybe the stuff contained steroids.'

'You're not taking this seriously, are you.' Meera puts the panel back, shaking bangles up her arm.

'Maybe you're taking it too seriously. Bugs and birds? Give me a fucking break.'

June and Ben look down into the building's vast central stairwell, a world of steel and concrete. A strong updraft ruffles their hair. June opens a pack of cigarettes and removes the silver foil from inside it. 'We're not even supposed to carry packets of cigarettes into the building,' she says, screwing the foil up into a ball and dropping it into the stairwell. It falls, then spins and hovers on the air current.

'Touch it.'

Ben gingerly touches the floating foil ball and gets an electric shock.

'The air flow is all messed up. It's like being in a funfair.'

In the corridor where they're standing, the wind moans eerily up the elevator shafts. Girls walk past, and their dresses lift in the updraft, like on a carnival walk.

'This is all bullshit; it's bad design, not bad vibes. You want to see a building with real problems? Visit the block of flats in Hackney where my old man lives. I'm going back –'

'Wait. You said you couldn't access the health records. Then at least you should talk to some of the staff. It's your job, Ben.'

'Damn. I thought I was going to get by on my looks.'

'You could start with Apela,' June tells him.

'Apela. Is that corporate jargon?'

'No, that's her first name. She's over there.'

'Okay, but if I'm not convinced, promise you'll drop the whole thing?'

'That's up to Miranda,' says June. She doesn't explain why.

Apela Tamarak is Fitch's PA. She moves her mobile phone closer to her computer, until it suddenly emits a piercing shriek. 'Watch,' she instructs Ben. The noise from the mobile subsides into an old pop song. It sounds like an early Manfred Mann hit, then there's a station ident from Radio Caroline.

'It keeps picking up old pirate radio shows from the sixties. How is that possible?'

They listen to the long-forgotten voices of the Radio Caroline DJs for a minute. Apela is enjoying the show. *Maybe she's nuts as well*, thinks Ben. He resolves to talk to some other staffers.

'I get these red dots before my eyes whenever I stare too long at the company screensaver,' says Alison, Clarke's PA. 'Then I pass out. Watch.'

Alison's head drops forward. She's out cold with her face on the desk. She opens one eye. 'Sometimes I pass out right on the keyboard. It leaves marks, you know?'

When she sits up, all her hair is standing on end.

Jake in Invoicing is more embarrassed about talking, but Ben is good with people. Finally he opens up. They're standing over a toilet in the men's room, staring into it. Jake grabs the handle and flushes.

'It flushes back to front,' Jake explains. 'The water goes down the hole anti-clockwise. It's only supposed to do that in Australia, isn't it?'

Harry, the mailboy, is happy to talk to anyone, particularly if they want to discuss shows on the Sci-Fi Channel. He points to some scratch-marks along the wall. 'There's, like, all this tiny graffiti everywhere. Check it out. Triple sixes, man. The mark of the beast. The ghost in the machine. Messages from another place. Warnings? Could be.' He shakes his head sadly. His hair wants washing. 'I get these weird headaches when I see them. Like something's trying to take control of my brain.'

'Do you smoke a lot of dope?' asks Ben.

Jake is puzzled. 'What's that got to do with it?'

Ben looks at his chaotic notes. None of them makes any sense. He studies the building blueprint, and reads the brochures. Words jump out: STATE OF THE ART – UNIQUE STRUCTURE – TWENTY NINE FLOORS OF NEW TECHNOLOGY

– *TWENTY NINE FLOORS* –

He cross-references the blueprint. Then he's walking through the building's lobby to a map of the floors. He has a readout of the building's blueprint in his hand. He looks at the map and counts the levels, running his finger up the panel. Twenty-nine. The blueprint says there are thirty.

He returns to his workstation, feeling beaten. As Miranda passes, he stops her. He has the feeling that he's getting involved, despite himself. He points out the notes he has taken.

'Buildings don't make people behave strangely,' he reasons, 'other people do. You really think there's something wrong with the place, or is this some new kind of urban myth?'

Miranda pulls a pen from behind her ear, displays it to Ben and places it halfway up the wall, where it stays. 'You tell me. Should it do that?'

They stand there looking at the pen as it starts to spin.

Ben decides to have a quiet word with Meera. 'Don't get me wrong,' he begins, 'I don't buy into any of this –'

Meera raises a pencilled eyebrow. 'But?'

'Okay, I went outside the building and counted the windows. There are meant to be twenty nine floors, but I counted thirty. Where's the extra floor, Meera?'

'Ah, now that's the big secret isn't it.'

'Meaning?'

'Meaning, first of all, that they didn't build a thirteenth floor. What you have here is a shrine to rationality built by irrational people. There are two floor twelves. Also, when I first joined, I went through the cabling with a fine-tooth comb and came up against a blank. I mean a real blank: a room that cables come in and out of, but nobody seems to know what's in there. Room 3014 ... but it's on the thirtieth floor. A floor that doesn't officially exist. But I've been up there. The door's always locked. Suppose it contains some kind of weird technology we're not allowed to know about? It's just sitting there, right above our heads.'

Suddenly they hear a rhythmic thumping noise and look up to see Clarke heading their way. Clarke stops by Meera's desk. Sweating and annoyed, the supervisor studies Ben as if he is some kind of peculiar biological anomaly. 'Mr Harper. Step into my office, would you?'

Clarke offers Ben a seat. The supervisor paces back and forth past his son's sports trophies. Clarke's elevated boot makes his clumping gait lop-sided. He is unpredictable when he's like this.

'I want you to know I was against your appointment here. But the law is on your side. You're here to fill a European requirement. You're a legal statistic.'

Ben shifts uncomfortably. 'I know it's only my first day, but it seems to me that people are experiencing low-level symptoms of illness, and they apparently think the building is at fault.'

'If someone comes to you with a problem, you report it to me.

Just stick to your job description and we'll get along fine. Don't give me bad news. I want solid factual evidence, not your vague opinions.'

Ben is already having a crisis of conscience. He wants to fit in, but he hates dishonesty. 'You expect me to falsify my findings?' That isn't what he meant to ask, but it's out now.

Clarke's eyes bulge unpleasantly as he looms close. He's been eating onions, and there's an under-scent of lard. 'Listen, you little prick, you stick to being a keyboard-monkey or I'll leave you twisting in the fucking wind. How clear is that?'

'Pretty clear. I'm just trying to do my job. I don't want to get the boot.' *That didn't go so well*, he thinks, not daring to look back as he leaves the office, mentally biting his fist.

A building like SymaxCorp is analogous to the backstage area of a theatre set. In the same way that Disneyland's miles of service corridors are not seen by the public, SymaxCorp's basement remains hidden from view. Beneath the lobby, spotlights reach off into the distance. Two servicewear-co-ordinated workmen study them.

'What are we looking for?' asks Tony Cox, not because he's interested but because it's nearly time to go home and he's starving.

'Damage from a power surge,' Ray Sturgiss, his supervisor, tells him. 'It came up on the board. I don't see any.'

'How do they keep everything so clean down here? You could eat off the fucking floor.' Tony snaps his gum and blows a bubble.

'Suction system removes all the dust. Howard's the only janitor for the whole building. One day, all places will be like this.'

'The hippy bloke? He never does any fucking work.'

As the workmen watch, the lights go out all the way along the corridor.

'Shit. That's a big one.' Ray looks up nervously. They descend and try the switches, but nothing happens. They flick on torches, illuminating a path. 'I don't understand. The system is brand new. There's nothing to go wrong.'

'Then where are the lights?' asks Tony.

28

'It must have damaged the sub-station.' They stop before a tall steel box, the door of which is raised. 'This shouldn't be open. It's hyper-sensitive equipment. It must have unsealed when the electrics crashed.'

Tony peers in. 'So what do we do?'

'Trip the relay from the mains after I've checked this.'

'Can you smell that? Something burning.' Tony sniffs the air.

'I've got no sense of smell, mate.' Ray rolls up his sleeves and reaches in to the rerouters. 'Was a time when they'd employ a bloke with a broom to keep a place clean. Now even a sweeper needs a fucking degree in electronics to figure out. Give me some light here. Tony? Coxie?' He looks around. Tony seems to have vanished. Suddenly, the lights come back on all the way along the corridor.

Relays trip. Electricity arcs. Machinery moves. The hum of new air starts up. Ray still has his hand inside the sub-station as the lid is reactivated and starts to close. There's no way he can get his hand out in time. He struggles, but the heavy steel lid is still coming down on his fingers.

'Coxie! Coxie! Shut it back off!' The metal sheet closes on his hand, crushing then snipping off his last two fingers at the first joint. Ray's agonised cries echo along the corridor, but his hand is free and the shield is back in place. The system's designed to do that, after all.

The built-up boot. You hear it coming from the other end of the corridor. You get to recognise the loping walk. Clarke clumps to the front of the seated workers and barks at them.

'Ladies and gentlemen,' he looks from one expectant face to the next, 'this Friday, SymaxCorp presents its office systems via the top floor satellite link to the New York Board Of Commerce. This will be the most important presentation in the company's history. The later you stay, the harder you work, the more likely you'll be to win promotion over your colleagues. Don't trust them, because they won't be trusting you. This isn't a business. It's a war that we intend to win. Get a good night's sleep. You have a very

29

tough week ahead of you.'

Ben and Miranda are seated near the back, like kids who talk in class. They eye each other with some suspicion. 'He should have been in the military,' says Ben.

'He *was*,' Miranda tells him. 'Desk job. The boot. But you never lose the discipline.'

Clarke is watching them.

3. TUESDAY

The building glints blackly beneath gathering storm clouds. Sometimes movement can be glimpsed within; it looks as though a great creature is shifting. The darkest part of the sky is touching the SymaxCorp roof. On the twentieth floor, Ben dons a headset and runs the SymaxCorp DVD he has been given. He finds himself watching more streams and woodland scenes. 'SymaxCorp creates integrated electronic office environments to suit any size of business ...' says a wholly insincere voice.

Ben wanders away through the open-plan floor. What should be ordinary is now becoming mysterious to him, because he sees it with fresh eyes.

A girl is on her hands and knees taping a cable along the floor.

A senior staffer is thumping his computer with his fist as the screen fills up with images from old porn films. John Holmes has a moustache, and is alternately fucking two overweight girls. The staffer is mortified with embarrassment.

'SymaxCorp sets new standards in office efficiency, allowing you to work – ' Here the DVD voiceover sticks and phases oddly, distorting. '– faster faster faster faster faster *faaaasterrrr* ... and better than the best from your staff ... no matter how urgent your deadline ...'

A secretary touches a scanner and her hair stands on end with static.

A worker is lying with his head on his desk. He is surrounded by aspirin packets and bottles.

Another secretary finds her cardigan sticking to the wall behind her. She pulls it free, but it floats away from her body again.

Ben examines a window covered with a spiral of small insects. He presses his hand against the glass and the insects drop away. He returns to his computer screen, where the DVD is still playing. The images are increasingly absurd and divorced from reality. He looks up and imagines the discreet ducts that supply air to the entire building, forming an X-ray of the building's walls, a maze of tubes he can hear hissing above his head as he works.

'... creating the ultimate electronic environment. One day this is how all first-world offices will operate ...'

Ben watches and listens, and gets jumpy despite himself. There's something wrong with his chair. It won't slide forward. The wheels keep catching on the carpet-square floor tiles. He bends down and looks closer. Someone has turned one of them around. He turns it back and finds he has pieced together a large brown bloodstain. What happened here? It seems a lot of blood for a paper cut.

Miranda catches up with him as he swipecards himself out. If he's honest with himself, he's been avoiding her all morning. 'Wait,' she calls, 'where are you going?'

'Outside, to get some fresh air. I've got a headache.'

'Did you know we have a garden here? Okay, it's kind of indoor, but it smells like real flowers. Really.' She smiles hopefully at him. She is – he has to admit – incredibly sexy. And she needs him.

The garden is in another part of the building's great atrium, an eerily pristine leisure area of walkways and flowers. No dogshit. No fag ends. Nothing real at all. It was built as an after-thought to the main building, once the architects realised that they had failed to provide any space where the staff could go to calm down. A completely secure leisure-area, a contradictory concept invented, unsurprisingly, in Los Angeles.

'Did you hear?' says Miranda. 'One of the electricians lost like his entire fucking arm or something last night. Industrial accident.

They fired him. Can you believe that? Negligence. They may even sue.' She seats herself on a green plastic park-bench affair. 'You've seen things for yourself, haven't you? Are you going to put them all in your report?'

Ben feels bloody-minded today. She pushes, he pulls, that kind of thing. 'All buildings have quirks,' he snaps. 'They're by-products of advanced technology.'

'The place is controlled by computers that purify the atmosphere.'

'Sounds like a good thing.'

'Not if they're killing you.'

Ben stops and turns on her. 'How do you know they are?'

'Come on, I know, all right?'

'But how?'

She decides. 'Felix told me about the radiation. It was in his report to Clarke.'

'If you're so damned sure you're being poisoned, why don't you tell the management?'

'Are you kidding? That's what he did. SymaxCorp has its own security staff. They're armed with Tasers. This is private property. It's outside police jurisdiction.'

'If you think it's so dangerous, maybe you should just leave.'

'That's what they want me to do. If you leave here, you get a black mark on your temp record that stays with you wherever you go. Nobody leaves unless they're forced to.'

Ben stops and looks at Miranda. She seems determined that he will help her, and he is equally determined to resist, although his determination is taking a few dents. But she's dangerous to know. Getting into trouble is the last thing he needs to do.

'I'm sorry,' he says finally. 'I've lost too many jobs for talking out of turn. This is my last chance. I can't let you screw it up.'

'And I've had enough jobs to know when something is fucked. Come with me.' She gets up and takes his hand. Looking around, she opens a door at the side of the lobby. It leads to a darkened stairwell where timer lights switch on. They walk down a ramp into the underground car park. It's gloomy, claustrophobic and concrete, with the kind of shiny floors that squeak as you turn the wheel.

'Someone's been scratching these all over the place,' Miranda explains, pointing out triple sixes surrounding a crucifix. She looks meaningfully at him. 'Evil besetting good. And they leave little notes. Look at this one: "GOD IS WATCHING YOU."' The words are scrawled all around the basement. In a shadowy corner stall stands a blue BMW covered in dust. 'You know I told you that Felix left his watch? That's nothing. He loved his car. He drove it into work but he never drove it home. Why would he have left it here?'

'What? What? You think the big bad corporation had him whacked? Do you realise how incredibly stupid that sounds?'

'He isn't at home, Ben. I checked with his neighbours. He hasn't been seen. He isn't anywhere.'

'Where are the car keys?'

Miranda hasn't thought of this. 'I think they were on his belt. On a ring with his flat keys. I know he had only one set.'

Ben stops. 'And how do you know that, exactly?'

'I just know, okay?'

'When was the last time you saw Felix?'

'He was working late, writing the report for Clarke.' They look up into the darkness of the basement roof, where the air ducts hiss. 'And he never left the building.'

'You want me to start nosing around for his sake?'

'No. I want you to do it for my sake.' She peels off her blue shirt and throws it over the TV camera. Then she removes her bra.

'Jesus, Miranda.'

'Let's keep religion out of this,' she warns, kissing him as she pushes him back across the hood of a car. Resistance is futile. He pulls her down on top of him. But before her nakedness fills his vision, he can't help but notice that the space they're in belongs to Clarke.

Later, they return to the garden. The river glistens like silver foil. Above them, a handful of stars have escaped the light pollution of the metropolis. But they are still behind the great glass wall, in the leisure area of the SymaxCorp atrium. Ben wonders if he will ever leave.

'Chaos and order,' he tells her. 'The universe has to be governed by one system or the other. The one you choose to believe in decides the kind of person you are.' He looks up through the glass at the night sky, at a blood-red moon. 'You can live in an entirely random way, going wherever you want, taking whatever work comes along – or you can build the world. I thought it was all about taking a stand. But it's about being part of something.' He says this admiringly as he tips back his head to look up at the illuminated rows of offices, each little box containing a person lost in concentration.

'I don't understand why you would choose to be a battery hen. Always knowing what's going to happen next.'

'I've tried the other way and it doesn't work,' he explains. 'One day you wake up and find you've done nothing with your time on Earth. This way I can make some money, start to create a future.'

'You think this is order? You think because you've entered corporate life, everything else is going to fall into place? This is chaos. That, up there, that's order.'

'At least my way I'll get a little respect.'

Miranda gives a derisive snort of laughter. 'You could spend twenty years here then get fired. Two days later, no-one would remember you.'

'You remember Felix.'

She stops laughing. 'I'm the only one who does. Ben, help me to find him.'

4. WEDNESDAY

Ben stands on the forecourt looking up at the building. He knows that his mood is darkening with every passing day, but what can you do? He signed up for the tour of duty. The clouds are even blacker now, and it is raining hard. London suits the rain, he thinks. Everyone goes indoors. He heads into the building with a fresh look of determination. Control is the key, he tells himself. Control.

He stays seated at his workstation for half an hour before Miranda looks furtively around and then wheels her chair over. Before she can speak, Ben holds up his hand to her. 'All right. All right. I'll find out what I can.' So much for his resolve. 'Tell me one thing. Last night ...'

'It wasn't because I wanted you to help me, all right? Happy?'

'Then what was it?'

'I like you. You have the kind of innocence a girl just wants to wreck.'

'You're not like anyone I've ever met before. '

'Is that good?'

'I don't know. Are you?'

She gives him a dirty smile. 'I could be better.'

'I just hope the cameras didn't pick us up.'

'You worry too much. What's the worst that could happen?'

'Never say that out loud.'

Through his window, Clarke silently observes them speaking. Checking his watch, he heads off to attend a meeting with the board, in a spectacular, hardwood, *faux*-19th Century conference room overlooking the city skyline. It would be wrong to think of the board members as villains. Nothing is as black and white as that anymore. They're a group of ordinary, hard-headed businessmen; but their luxurious private world is cocooned, far away from the floors below. They no longer empathise, because they're dealing now in abstract concepts. The world of business management would rather think about *pluralistic environments* than toilet dispensers.

'This deal will turn us into the global standard,' Clarke promises. 'It'll allow us to showcase systems in government buildings all over the world. I'll have to push the staff hard. We'll have to go through the night.'

'Does this mean paying overtime?' asks the company's chief accountant.

'I don't see how we can legally avoid that.'

'What you're asking us is –'

Clarke interrupts. 'I want your permission to go into Room 3014.' The directors look at one another in trepidation, but they already know it's necessary.

Ben checks the floor buttons, and takes the lift to the twelfth floor. He gets out and looks around. An unmarked door leads to another staircase. Climbing the steps, he arrives at a new floor. Apparently there really are two twelfth floors.

Returning to the lift, he heads up to the twenty ninth floor. Another unmarked door leads upwards. He emerges into a dimly lit corridor, plushly-carpeted. At one end of the corridor, he sees a door of polished steel, stencilled as Room 3014. Putting his ear to the cold metal, he hears a low hum emanating from within.

He turns around and walks straight into a tall, cadaverous man in a black suit. Even the senior staff call him Dracula, because he's the spit-double of Christopher Lee, and he's never been seen outside of the building in daylight. That's as far as their imaginations stretch.

'What are you doing here?' asks Dr Hugo Samphire, the

Chairman of SymaxCorp. 'This floor is for the exclusive use of the board members.'

'Dr Samphire. I got lost.'

'You should have memorised the building plan in your company bible.'

'I did, but this floor isn't on it.'

'Need to know, Mr ...' He squints at Ben's badge. 'Harper. Go back to your workstation and do whatever it is we pay you too much to do.'

But he doesn't. Instead, he meets Miranda in another part of the steel and glass atrium. This part is *faux*-jungly and filled with tall palms that seem real. Miranda lights a cigarette, with her patented *Fuck 'em* attitude. People back away from her, because smoking is a sackable offence.

'I'm not near the sensors, okay? They would set the alarms off. I know where they all are. It helps me to think.' She blows smoke discreetly. 'Clarke is tripling everyone's workload in order to meet Friday's deadline. After this, all leave is cancelled.'

'What, you think you can't handle the pressure?'

'I'm used to hard work, sonny. What's the matter with you?'

'It's bullshit about the thirtieth floor. There's no mystery to it. There's a bigger problem here.'

'What do you mean?'

'I studied the sick lists. There's a sharply rising pattern of illnesses. I'm down to see Willis, the staff nurse.'

Miranda throws him a look. 'Good luck. You'll need it.'

Willis is middle-aged, and exhausted about it. The staff nurse sits in the building's medical centre, sticking nicotine patches up her arm. 'Care for a nicotine patch?' she offers. 'They're great. I always have one around about now.'

'No thanks. How's business?'

'Don't ask. I can't sew fingers on, for Christ's sake. One of the workmen lost two of them.'

'I guess you must have noticed this.' Ben shows her a graph of rising sicknesses reported by staff. 'Headaches. Hallucinations.

Mental problems. That's a lot of strange behaviour.'

Willis keeps sticking, barely bothering to look up. 'Staff will tell you it's stress-related. That's bollocks. Ask someone if they work too hard, they're not going to say no, are they? Everyone's under stress; it shouldn't make that much difference. Nobody smokes or drinks anymore. They should; it'd calm them down. I suppose it might be SBS. Sick Building Syndrome. Except that the building's constructed from hypoallergenic materials.'

'Something must be causing this. So many of the women ...'

'The female staff don't operate collectively, Mr Harper. We're not nuns. We don't all get our period at the same time. But there is something, some kind of psychosoma.'

'What do you mean?'

'I dunno, it's hard to pinpoint. Natural tendencies get exaggerated under pressure. The sickly ones get sick, the angry ones lose their tempers more, the depressed ones get melancholy. There are chemicals that will do that, but there's no reason for them being used here.'

'Has anyone ever tested for them?'

'Not to my knowledge.'

'Can you get me data on anything you think qualifies as unusual behaviour?'

'Sure. I managed to find quite a lot for Felix.'

'So what happened to the report?'

She studies him with hooded eyes. 'What do you think?'

It's early afternoon, and the atmosphere on Ben's floor is ramping up. People are tense and visibly working faster. In the reception area, the video images and soothing music now play at a faster, more urgent pace. Ben sits at his computer trying to access Felix's files. He discovers a set of dated reports:

CONTENTS DELETED
CONTENTS DELETED
CONTENTS DELETED

He stretches out his back, then looks around and sees Fitch shouting at June and throwing papers onto the floor.

'You collate the forms in binders, not with these damned things! It's not hard to remember.' Fitch looks exasperated. June is forced to bend and pick everything up.

June mutters under her breath. It sounds like she says: 'Fitch the bitch.'

'We don't have to hire the obese, you know. We're doing you a favour. You can keep this job or just order yourself more dessert.' Fitch clutches her forehead, as if in pain. Ben frowns. Even from the little he knows about Fitch, this is uncharacteristically cruel. She's obviously been drinking. He had her down as more professional. June's nearly in tears. Ben can't stand by and do nothing, even though it means breaking his vow. 'What is your problem?' he asks Fitch.

'Inefficiency is my problem, Mr Harper. We get this done right, we win the contract and we all get to keep our jobs. We may even get bonuses at Christmas. Things are going to get a lot tougher around here. You want to be a lightweight, tell me you can't handle the pressure.'

'Ben, don't, it doesn't matter,' June interrupts, anxious for her new colleague not to cause a scene.

'Look,' Ben tells Fitch, 'if she's suffering from stress-related illness, she can report it to me and I'll take action for her – until then, sober up and back off.' He storms back to his station in anger.

'I like you like that,' Miranda whispers.

'Well, I don't like myself like that.'

'Fitch has been getting at June all week, but I've never seen her like this before.'

Clarke sees them talking and calls Ben over with a curt: 'Harper. My office. Now.'

When Ben comes into the office, Clarke stalks around him in a predatory, unsettling manner. 'Do yourself a favour. Stay away from Jameson. She's good at her job. But she's trouble.'

Ben finds himself defending her. 'Miranda's concerned about my predecessor getting dismissed.'

'Of course she's concerned. She was going out with him. When she broke it off, he was so upset that he had to leave. He couldn't

40

bear to keep seeing her.'
Ah. That would explain it.

Miranda runs to catch up with him. He's leaving for the night. Ben keeps walking.

'Hey, wait for me. I thought we were spending the evening together.'

'You didn't tell me you were going out with Felix.'

'Did Clarke tell you that? We had a one night stand, all right?'

'You dumped him.'

'Bullshit. He ended it, not me.'

'He couldn't stay any longer because he felt uncomfortable around you.'

'Clarke's trying to divide us, don't you see? I'm just worried about him. Clarke knows what happened. There has to be a way to make him admit the truth. You know it's the right thing to do.'

'Yeah, that's what I usually get fired for. Doing the right thing.' Ben carries on, leaving her behind. He doesn't want to be angry with her, but the devil in him won't forgive. She catches him up.

'Ben, I'm not using you. I wouldn't do that. I think you're … I don't know. You care. You'll make a difference whatever you do. I liked Felix a lot. Now I've no-one else. Please Ben.'

The devil wins. Ben leaves for the night. Miranda can do nothing but watch him go.

Up on the twentieth floor, senior manager Meadows sits in a glass box like Clarke's, ploughing through piles of paperwork while working two computer screens and taking three calls, crazy-busy. His assistant, Jo Cousins, a battle-tough woman in her fifties, puts her head around the door. 'New York's on Line 2, Mr Meadows, and your wife's still holding on 3.'

'I told you to tell her I'll call back,' Meadows hisses. He takes a call, then another, wipes his forehead and examines the flickering call switches, buzzes his assistant. 'Hold all my calls, Cousins.'

'I can't. New York is urgent, I can't keep –'

41

'Hold the fucking calls!'

Meadows rises and locks Cousins out of the office. For a moment, he thinks he can smell burning. Then he methodically turns off the computer screens and tears the phone jacks out of the wall. He puts on a CD – 'Barcarolle' from 'The Tales Of Hoffmann' – and cranks the music up high. Next, he begins to take off his clothes, neatly folding each item – shirt, tie, trousers – on his desk.

His flustered assistant sees what is happening and tries the door of the office. Meadows' behaviour attracts the attention of others.

Now completely naked, the supervisor goes to the window and strikes it with a chair. He has to do this six times before the glass cracks. Cousins hammers on the glass wall as others try to break the office door down.

As the music reaches its height, Meadows climbs out onto the window ledge. He is naked, and has cut himself badly on the broken glass. Meadows' eyes cloud over a milky white. He braces himself, then swan-dives, out into the sky and the streets below, sailing, sailing all the way down to his death.

There is a rending of flesh and glass as Meadows' body explodes through the canopy above the station platforms, and home-going commuters scream and run.

5. THURSDAY

The building's security guards have roped off the area around the shattered window. It's stormier than ever outside, raining grey pellets. Normal work has been disrupted as everyone talks about what has happened. There are boards around Meadows' office that only serve to draw attention to it.

Ben passes Willis with a dry, knowing look. 'You said you'd get me data if there was unusual behaviour. I think that constitutes "unusual behaviour", don't you?'

Willis guiltily agrees with a sigh. 'Meet me for lunch. I'll have your data for you.'

Puzzled, Ben looks through the door to Meadows' shattered window, then walks back through the open-plan floor to his desk. *What the fuck is going on?* he wonders.

Two male office workers are having a violent argument about – it seems – pens. A girl is crying quietly at her workstation. Others seem to be suffering from bad headaches. One is staring into an empty waste-basket as if searching for the meaning of life.

Ben watches Miranda working, her tongue poking from the side of her mouth in concentration. Suddenly smitten, he draws a red love-heart on a piece of paper and folds it into an aeroplane. He remembers how to do this from his last job as a carer.

He launches the paper plane at Miranda's desk. It hovers for a moment, then gets sucked into the wall grating between them. If he concentrates hard, he can actually see the air in the room. It's like the building is respiring.

Miranda feels him looking. She glances up and smiles. Checking the coast is clear, she comes over to speak to him. 'What do you think about Meadows going for a walk in the clouds? The official line is that he was under a lot of pressure and had a nervous breakdown. Some breakdown. They had to hose him off the platform. They found his teeth in McDonalds –'

Suddenly Ben looks sick and disorientated.

'What's the matter?'

'Nothing. I feel a little weird. I need to go to the bathroom.' Once there, Ben is violently, volubly sick. He soaks a paper towel in cold water and presses it against his forehead. Hearing rhythmic noises, he turns and sees a couple, Alison and another office worker, making intense love in one of the open toilet cubicles, their bouncing, fleshy images distorted in the mirror. Now they are photographing each other and laughing. Ben looks at his watch. 'It's ten o'clock in the morning. Jesus, get a room.'

Spotting a slew of discarded photographs lying across the floor, he picks them up and studies them.

Perspiring and pale, he walks with Miranda. 'You okay?' she asks.

'Better than the others.' He points to their fellow workers, some mumbling, rocking in their chairs, clutching their heads like lunatics in Bedlam. Others are simply eyes-down and working hard, just as they always have.

'Clarke had most of the division working all night. Not me, thank God. Temps charge too much overtime.' They pass the photocopying/scanning room, where a girl is sitting on the photocopier, running out pictures of her arse. 'She's been doing that for nearly an hour. I wouldn't mind, but I've got some photocopying to do. What did Willis say?'

'I'm meeting her in the restaurant. Does everything seem strange to you? I mean really strange?'

'Hallelujah, he sees the light. C'mere.' She grabs his face and kisses him.

'I've seen a lot more than the light. Take a look at these. They were in the bathroom.' He hands Miranda the set of Polaroids. 'The staff seem to have spent part of last night photographing each other naked.' He calls out to the passing Swan, who looks harassed. 'Mr Swan, would it be possible to have a word with you?'

Ben follows Swan into his office and shuts the door. He shows him the photos. Swan seems confused and distracted. Perhaps he, too, is losing control.

'What do you make of these?'

'You should have seen it here last night.' Swan mops his forehead with a paper tissue, leaving little bits stuck to his skin. 'And now look. Fights breaking out. People being rude to one another. Tasteless remarks made toward our non-Caucasian staff. Dirty pictures scrawled on the walls of the toilets. It's against nature and it's against God.'

'It's time to do something about this – maybe even evacuate the building until we can figure out –'

But Swan isn't listening. He's got his hands on a Bible and is brandishing it. '*For the Lord sayeth, Be not overcome with evil, but overcome evil with good. Romans 12:21.* Someone has to keep a watch on this place.' He whispers disconcertingly in Ben's ear. 'The Devil is in control of this building.'

'It was you who put the triple sixes and crucifixes all around the basement?'

'We have to warn the innocent, don't you understand? You'll pray with me, won't you? Say you'll get on your knees and pray!'

Ben manages to excuse himself and get out of the office. He heads for the reception area.

The video screens have all been changed again. Instead of streams and wheatfields, they now show fast industrial machinery shots cut to hard hip-hop beats.

'Who changed the screens?' he asks, as he passes.

'Mr Clarke's orders,' the receptionist tells him. 'Inspires the workforce, paces things up. It's like being stabbed in the ears with red hot needles. Can you get repetitive brain injury?' She drops her head back onto her console with a thud.

Willis looks furtive and distraught as she leafs through her notes.

Ben notices she has a number of chewed-up pencils in her hair. Her nicotine patches have increased in size. 'Look, maybe I was wrong,' she admits. 'Maybe it is stress-related. The business with Meadows has freaked everyone. There's been a big rise in health problems among workers with a history of migraine, asthma or any kind of mental disturbance. I ran medical data matches on key personnel to find out who would be most susceptible. Guess who came out top?'

Easy one. 'Mr Clarke.'

'How did you know? He has a history of anger-management problems going back a long way. I think he may be – unwell.'

The pair become aware of a ruckus going on by the food counter. June is trying to return her lunch-plate to an upset chef. 'You taste it, it's tainted,' she explains, visibly upset.

'You don't know what you're talking about,' the chef rallies. 'I made it fresh this morning.' One of the other diners is eating, and suddenly throws up. Others start gagging and vomiting. The restaurant quickly becomes disgusting. Everyone is being sick. The air is suddenly sour with bile. Ben pushes around to the back of the counter. 'Health and Safety. Could you show me where you prepared it?'

The chef leads the way to the rear of the kitchen, where a brushed-steel electronic panel is the master-control for the kitchen. 'Everything is automated, see? The quantities are mixed here. All I have to do is program them in. Nothing is touched by human hand.' Everything's spotlessly clean, but Ben becomes aware of a terrible smell in this area. 'Christ, what is that?' he asks.

He looks up at the vent above the master-control. It connects to a thick steel tube. He pulls a refrigeration unit out of the way. Something disgusting is leaking out of the tube. It leads directly over the food container. 'What's that for?'

'Hot air convector; it keeps the food at a preset temperature.'

Ben grabs a spanner and breaks the tube apart. He quickly wishes he hadn't; it's full of liquid shit. Everyone jumps back, horrified, as the floor is spattered.

'Where is this supposed to lead?'

'Just to the boiler.'

From up the vent, through square steel ducts, through all manner of pipes and tunnels, the effluent sweeps, driven by pumps. Ben runs upstairs, following the ductwork. Behind him follows Miranda. The last duct leads to a junction, where the toilet waste pipe has been connected to the hot air intake. Both pipes are clearly labelled. Ben smashes them apart. Somebody has rerouted the pipes with silver racing tape. It's an act of vandalism.

'Why would anyone do that?' asks Miranda.

'To be a force of chaos.' Ben looks at her. 'To wreck the system.'

'You don't think – I wouldn't even know where to begin ...'

Ben studies her long and hard. He softens. 'All right. Let's go and see someone who would know where to begin.'

Ben and Miranda head down to the basement. 'Seriously, why would someone join the pipes together?' Miranda keeps asking him, as if he can explain everything that's going on. 'Industrial espionage?'

'That's about ripping off patents, not poisoning everyone in the building. It doesn't make sense. This guy Howard is in charge of building maintenance. Willis warned me that he's sort of – unusual.'

They arrive on a Hawaiian beach at sunset. Palm-fringed sands, ukulele music playing on a stereo somewhere, over the sloshing of small waves. Howard the janitor is sitting in a deckchair in sunglasses, before a sun-lamp and back-projected video screens. There's sand all over the floor, plus a few seashells. He's dressed in a Hawaiian shirt and shorts, and is drinking a Mohito mixed in a coconut.

'No point in getting stressed,' he drawls, in his medicated-for-the-hell-of-it voice. 'Electromagnetic pulses. Radiation that fries your brain, man. There are phones, computers and monitors in every square inch of this place. They don't even know what effect it has on humans, but you can see what it does to things with simple nervous systems. Check out the bugs, man.' He points his sandal at a ring around his work area, where hundreds of cockroaches lie in piles. 'Works on pigeons, too. Anything with a tiny brain.'

'Do you think it could trigger some kind of reaction in humans?' asks Miranda.

'That's science-fiction bollocks. All it does is damage cells. It explains the insects and the pigeons. They drop when they hit a certain radius around the building.'

'But it doesn't come close to explaining what's happening in here,' says Ben.

Howard has no answer for that.

Clarke is on the prowl, and notices the two empty workstations. He stops by Meera's desk. 'Where are they?' he demands, smoothing down his combover, something that is fast becoming a nervous tic.

'I asked them to give me a hand, sir,' Meera volunteers. 'I had too much to do by myself.'

'Well, get them back, before you find yourself with nothing to do ever again.' Clarke continues to snoop around Ben's workstation, and starts fooling around with his computer. There's a private file on the desktop. Clarke clicks it open. He finds himself looking at the original, untampered-with version of Ben's CV, including his terminated employments and a note:

HOSPITALISATION: NERVOUS EXHAUSTION

Clarke mutters to himself. The little prick has never held down a job in his life. He picks up the nearest phone, eyeing his wall-mounted cricket bat. 'Security? I want you to track down a member of staff for me. Ben Harper. When you find him, bring him to my office.'

At that moment, Howard is showing Miranda and Ben the building's plans on his laptop. 'There's more electronic resonance in this building than in any yet designed,' he explains. 'It's fucking with the laws of nature, man. And they want to put them up everywhere.'

This doesn't make sense to Ben. Too vague, too neat. 'So you get some electrical disturbance – that wouldn't make people act crazy, would it?'

'We've no idea how the brain works except for electrical activity. Maybe there's an interdimensional element. Maybe we're on an old burial ground. Who knows what bad karma lies under the city streets? Spooky, eh?'

Ben and Miranda look at him in some annoyance. Ben is feeling terrible. He's sweating hard and looking greenish. 'Then why isn't everyone affected?'

'Physiology. Some skulls are thicker than others. And some people have weaknesses. You know, past problems. Hey, you don't look so good.'

Miranda's mobile rings. 'Meera? Shit.' She turns to Ben. 'You left the original version of your CV on your desktop.' As she's speaking, a pair of large and fantastically stupid security guards come into the basement. Their uniforms are stretched at the stomach buttons.

'Harper, you have to come with us now,' says the first, thrilled to be delivering a line he's heard in countless movies. Ben hesitates for a moment, then makes a run for it. Howard points towards the back of the sunset cyclorama.

Ben finds himself in the fire escape. He races up the stairs as fast as he can. As the pursuing guards close in, Ben ducks out onto one of the other floors.

People are behaving as if they've been drugged. They barely notice Ben as he pushes through them. The guards seem to have become distracted by a young woman who has taken her top off. As he escapes, Ben ducks back into the main stairwell and hides in one of the toilets. It's not exactly heroic, but it gets him out of a situation.

In the next cubicle, an executive sits crying his eyes out. The atmosphere in the building has now phased beyond the grasp of normality. But it's a closed world. Outside, everyone goes about their work. Nobody really knows what goes on in other people's offices.

The guards enter the toilet. When Ben looks around the door, he is caught. After a brief struggle, he's overpowered.

The stony-faced security team lead Ben back up to Clarke's

twentieth-floor office. When he ducks and tries to escape, they punch him viciously in the stomach. Clarke is waiting at his computer.

'Mr Harper,' he says pleasantly, 'do have a seat.' He waves the guards away. 'I don't think you've been very honest with us about your career. Let's take a look, shall we?' He takes great pleasure in punching up Ben's CV.

Ben tries to catch his breath. He knows he is seconds from being thrown out of the building, and there's nothing he can do. The file takes forever to open. Clarke waits. Outside, Meera anxiously transfers documents, cutting and pasting. When Clarke's file opens, the supervisor sees that it has been completely revised. Furious, he jumps up and drags Ben out to his own workstation, where he punches up the same file, only to get the same result.

Clarke is staggered. He knows he's been had, and hates it. 'I don't know how you did this, pal, but I'll find out,' he screams, his voice cracking. 'Nobody pisses in my gravy and gets away with it.'

Meera walks behind Clarke, smiling as she slips the disk into her pocket. The supervisor turns to the rest of the staff, who are watching him anxiously. 'Get on with your work, all of you.' He turns on Miranda. 'And you, get back to your job or …'

'What will you do, kick me out? You can't fire me, Hopalong, I'm not permanent.'

'You'll be here tomorrow if you want to work in this city ever again.' With that, Clarke strides angrily away.

Ben pulls Miranda aside. 'We need to get to the directors. If there is something going on, they have to be told.'

'They already know, Ben. All they care about is making money.'

'Oh, I get it, evil corporation takes over world. It must be so easy going through life with that good/bad thing going on in your head.'

'You think they don't know that something is wrong with the system? How can you be so naive?'

'I nearly just got fired because I was downstairs listening to Howard explain about altered dimensions.'

50

'So you're not going to help me find Felix's report?'

'I didn't say that.' Ben touches his sore stomach, knowing that a point has been passed. 'We'll search the office tonight.'

The building looks silvery against a dark sky. The office lights are still on, but most of the staff, including Clarke, have left. Ben and Miranda wait while Fitch shuts down her computer. 'You can go home now,' she says suspiciously, 'both of you.'

'We have some work to finish, Miss Fitch.' Miranda smiles unconvincingly.

'You know you're not supposed to remain on the premises without a supervisor.'

Miranda holds up a sheaf of paper, making sure Fitch can't see that the pages are blank. 'Mr Clarke specifically asked for these to be finished tonight.'

'Well ... all right. But remember, you're being recorded.'

Ben and Miranda wait for Fitch to leave, then head for Clarke's office. Ben stands on a chair and takes a digital photograph of Clarke's office from an angle just below the CCTV camera. He plugs the camera into his computer and opens the CCTV camera's digital file. 'Meera showed me how to do this,' he explains, replacing the current digital feed with the file he's just shot. It looks identical.

Miranda watches, amazed. 'And to think you didn't know how to turn a computer on four days ago.' They enter Clarke's office. Miranda searches the cupboards while Ben boots up Clarke's terminal.

But Clarke has only reached the lobby doors. It is raining hard. He looks up at the sky, and turns back. His umbrella is still propped up in the corner of his office.

Ben and Miranda can't find anything. Ben's run of luck with technology ends as the computer sounds an intruder alert. And Clarke is coming up in the elevator. They frantically try to shut down the computer, but it starts deleting the hard drive, file by file.

'I knew I shouldn't have touched it,' wails Ben, watching as the screen scrolls and wipes. 'It's clearing the whole lot.'

Clarke arrives at his floor and steps out of the elevator. He lopes noisily toward his office. He's maybe thirty seconds away.

Ben watches helplessly as file after file is destroyed in total meltdown. In desperation, Miranda pulls the plug on the whole system.

Ben hears Clarke coming. He shoots Miranda a horrified look and drags her behind the door. Clarke steps inside and stops. He reaches down for his umbrella and pauses, sensing something amiss. Ben and Miranda hold their breath. Clarke is a fairytale wolf sniffing the air for humans. Time stretches into an agonised intake of breath.

But he goes. Ben kisses Miranda in relief, but she returns his kiss passionately. *Perhaps she gets off on this, but it's killing me*, he thinks. 'Do you reckon we'll ever get to do this somewhere else?' asks Ben, as they surface.

Miranda does her mischief face. 'I thought you enjoyed danger.'

'I'd enjoy horizontal.'

Rain is illuminated on the tall glass walls as they slow to a walk across the foyer. Miranda thinks aloud. 'Well, if Clarke had the report file, he certainly doesn't have it now.'

'Then we'll get to the truth another way.'

Miranda suddenly spins around and kisses him hard. 'I can't deal with this place any longer. I've decided, I'm not coming back next week.' Ben stares at her in astonishment. 'You don't need this job, either. You don't have to take a stand. Look what it does to people.'

'You're right, Miranda. I don't need this job.' He feels suddenly lighter. 'Fuck, we can go anywhere we want.'

'Tahiti.'

'Tasmania.'

'Alexandria.'

'Istanbul.'

'Cardiff.'

'The Cote D'Azur. *Cardiff?*'

'Spend the weekend with me,' pleads Miranda. 'Tomorrow'll

be my last day, then I'll be free. Let's celebrate. To corporate sabotage ...'

'And the death of big business.'

Miranda is right. He's come a long way in four days.

6. FRIDAY 9:25 AM

The stormy weather has been building all week. Now the heat cracks, and thunder riffs around the office towers, hitting the business district in full fury. Cauls of rain wash across the bare quadrangles. Sheets of water slam and break around planes of windswept concrete. The workers scurry into the sheltering cathedral of the SymaxCorp building under black umbrellas. Religious places are always places of refuge as well as of torment.

Ben shakes out his umbrella, besmirching the perfect marble of the lobby floor with dark spots. He catches Meera near the elevator and steers her away from the gaze of the cameras. He wants to thank her for the helping hand yesterday. Miranda tick-tocks her way across the lobby toward them. She's already been in for a couple of hours.

'Today's the big one,' Meera warns. 'They've been working all night again. I feel fucking awful and I haven't even been here.' It feels weird to hear a girl in a sari swear. They both recognise that there's a crisis coming, but what can they do? They're merely paid employees. Even nicknaming the Chairman after a vampire is tantamount to civil disobedience, and it's as far as most of their colleagues will dare go. But multinational conglomerates are not taken down by the judicious wielding of sarcasm. There aren't even many directors, thinks Ben, who can make policy changes. When a company gets this big, it becomes a machine with a mind of its own.

The lift arrives. There's a girl inside who can't decide whether to come out or stay in. She drops a pile of papers, looking half-dead. 'Some people upstairs are getting very fucking weird,' she says, as Ben, Meera and Miranda pile in. 'Three o'clock this morning, there was a fist-fight between two teams over *coffee-breaks*.'

'Why do they stay?' asks Ben.

'Hive mentality,' Meera tells him. 'We're worker bees, conditioned from birth. That, and the incredible overtime.'

'Why do we live this shitty life when we could be lying in the sun?' asks the girl, not looking as if she expects an answer. 'I haven't had a tan since student riots closed our school.'

'Clarke came in at five o'clock this morning,' Miranda yawns. 'He's having a shit-fit about his computer. His entire hard drive has gone.' She flashes a furtive smile at Ben. 'I'm out of here the second I get paid.'

The morning starts bad and gets worse. Clarke is ensconced in his office with the door shut. Every once in a while, a muffled shout of anger comes through the wall. The work-floor is a mess. There are papers, files and half-eaten boxes of junk food everywhere. Someone has thrown their trousers into the fountain.

At eleven, Miranda grabs Ben and drags him off. 'You have got to come and see this.' She leads him down a floor, to the Accounts Department, and pushes open a door.

'Apparently, they've been here all night. No wonder Meadows took a dive.'

The accountants are gathered around a computer that they have covered in dozens of red candles and votive offerings. They appear to be worshipping it, chanting numbers at the garlanded screen. Their hummed refrain is the theme tune to *The Simpsons*.

'It's true,' says Ben. 'There is a thin line between accountancy and madness.'

At eleven thirty, Meera makes an announcement. 'I think I've been looking for the wrong thing,' she tells them, tapping her screen with a pen.

'What do you mean?'

'Electro-magnetic radiation wouldn't do this. You heard

Howard. I've been on every website he could recommend and haven't found a thing. It couldn't spark a kind of collective mental breakdown.'

'So what do we look for?'

'I don't know – some kind of trauma event.'

'When did you first notice changes in people?'

Miranda thinks. 'Maybe three weeks ago.'

'Soon after Felix went missing. You're sure he never went home? Suppose he's still here.' Ben feels tired and sore-headed. He didn't sleep well.

'There is one way to find out,' suggests Meera.

'How?'

'His car key has a finder. It emits an electronic pulse coded to its matching base. All staff with car park spaces have them. It's so the guards can locate the keys to move vehicles.'

Miranda slaps her forehead. 'I didn't know that. I didn't know that! I'm sorry, I don't drive, all right?'

'How will we find the key finder?' asks Ben.

'It'll be with the rest of Felix's things,' says Miranda. 'I can take care of the search. What are you two going to do?'

'We're going to get Clarke's keys,' says Ben, 'and take a look inside Room 3014.'

7. FRIDAY 11:47 AM

It's a drastic move, but she can't think what else to do: Meera chucks a cup of coffee into a wiring panel and shorts the computer outside Clarke's office. Then she calls Fitch's attention to the computer. Fitch is drunker than a fly in a martini. She hammers on Clarke's door, and he emerges, looking as if he's just been woken up. The moment he leaves his office to inspect the damage, Ben slips inside, searching his jacket for keys. He's out with them just before Clarke storms back, slamming the door behind him.

Across the room, Miranda is going through Felix's desk. She locates the key finder, a black plastic hand-set, and turns it on, so that its LED starts slowly chirping.

She sets off to find out where the sound is coming from, running the finder around the room. The electronic signal quickens – especially when she moves near a large aluminium ventilator grating.

She sees another CCTV camera secreted on the floor in the corner of the room. You'd think the damn things were breeding. She twists the entire unit off its base and throws it in a bin. The finder is going mad. Miranda pulls out a screwdriver and starts undoing the screws that hold the vent cover.

Far above her, on the forbidden directors' floor, Ben and Meera step out into the corridor. They head for Room 3014. The door has warning signs on it:

HAZCHEM, STERILE ZONE.

Fumbling with the keys, Meera checks her back, then opens

the great steel door.

They slip inside and find, in the centre of the room, an immense, grey plastic box. There are a number of unmarked yellow cylinders, like diving tanks, connected to it.

Ben is disappointed. 'That's the sensor unit for an air-con system.'

Meera shakes her head. 'This isn't any old air-con system, baby, it's a SymaxCorp system. This is what we make. I've never seen one of these things up close.'

'What's the difference?'

'What's the difference between a Ford and a Ferrari? This is the future. Check it out. The chemical composition of the building's atmosphere can be changed via different program settings. When people get tense, they breathe quicker, and you get excess acidity in the air. The gauges measure dioxins and alkaline levels and gently compensate, restoring a natural oxygen balance that relieves stress. Except ...' She checks a line of coloured bars, incomprehensible to Ben.

'Except what?'

'These readings are way off. The SymaxCorp system doesn't just recycle air from outside, it adds pure oxygen. But this isn't pure. It's some kind of weird chemical mix. I know enough about pharmacology to see that half of this shit isn't even approved for public consumption.' She runs her hand along some greyish residue at the outlet to one of the pumps, and licks her index finger. 'Interesting.'

'What?'

'I think we've got one superheated cocaine speedball going through the building. Mix it with a cocktail of manufactured chemical compounds, and there's no telling what the effects could be. How long can you hold your breath?'

'Everyone has to breathe.' They consider the point for a moment. 'You think the directors figured they could get everyone to work harder if they pumped in this stuff?'

'Long-term, it would brain-damage your workforce. That would be counter-productive. Wouldn't it?'

58

'Then they must have introduced the crack element in order to get the presentation prepared in time.'

'So how is all the other stuff getting mixed in there?'

'Maybe the system is fucked.'

They look at the gleaming pipes and cylinders, and listen to the insidious hiss of air.

Miranda takes the vent casing off and climbs inside the duct. She enters an unnerving maze of tubes, tunnels and conduits. The dark passages get narrower as she follows the quickening chirrup of the finder, pushing her way into ever more claustrophobic spaces. Following the signal, she turns into another pipe with a smaller gauge –

– and discovers that she is stuck. No matter how hard she wriggles, she can't free herself from the constricting walls of the pipe. The key-finder is beeping faster still.

Ben and Meera, meanwhile, have torn up a floor grating in Room 3014 and are now, coincidentally, peering down into another of the interconnected vents. Meera is trying to make sense of what she's seeing. Why would the system radically change the air?

Miranda is starting to panic. She is completely trapped. There's no way forward and no way back. The key-finder is going wild, almost a continuous beep. She twists in the hot darkness, and finds a loose steel plate above her. She manages to raise her foot and kick at the plate. It's not bolted, and flies away.

Felix's rotting corpse falls on top of her.

Miranda screams, fighting off the maggot-infested cadaver as it leaks over her neck and arms, its putrefying face falling against hers, its stomach bursting open in a liquefied mess, releasing its gases. Fumes roll off the body, travelling up through the ventilation shafts, all the way to the sensors in Room 3014 …

… which go wild as they try to rebalance the air composition.

The sensors react to the rotting cadaver, sending chemical gauges into red-zone overload.

An electronic alarm starts whining somewhere. Lights flash. It's never a good sign when systems in public places do this.

Bathed in pulsing crimson light, Ben and Meera see the startling effect on the sensors. They are connected to tanks of air additives, the mechanical valves of which start rotating. Now they are unstoppably turning by themselves, until they are wide open.

'Whoa!' Meera jumps back. 'Something big just hit the sensors.'

'Was it something we did?'

'I think we should get out of here.' The pair of them duck out of the room, shutting the door behind them.

Above Swan's desk, next to his framed Bible quotes, a sensor light starts pulsing red. Newly toxic air is pumping out of the vent above him. He's sweating, and Bible-thumping mad.

Above Clarke's head, too, a sensor light starts pulsing as poisoned air pours through the vent in an unpleasantly warm stream.

Above Fitch's head, an identical sensor light pulses as the deadly air pumps in more heavily than ever before.

Air vents above all of the remaining working staff start to deliver corrupt air as the remaining green LEDs switch over to red.

In the security guards' station, the same thing is happening. Poisoned air pumps in, and red lights flash. One guard pulls his Taser from his holster, and cracks it into life with a wicked grin.

All over the building, the air is being replaced.

8. FRIDAY 12:07 PM

Miranda desperately hammers on the wall of the pipe. The matching key on Felix's collapsed, putrid body is flashing with the finder. She can't move back because the corpse is blocking her exit. There's no way of moving forward. The air is clouding up, getting hard to breathe.

Through every floor, staff members are feeling the effects of the contaminated air. Collars are torn open, work is stamped on and thrown into bins – it's an effect they have been feeling for weeks, but infinitely multiplied.

Clarke comes out of his office, looking crazed. He sees Ben's, Meera's and Miranda's empty workstations. 'Where are they?' he asks, in his softest, most menacing tone. 'What the bloody hell is going on around here?' He ignores the fact that half his staff seem to be missing. That's the trouble with obsessives; they home in on one thing and won't leave it alone. 'Young people think they're so clever,' he rants. 'We'll see about that. Why is there no discipline in this office?'

Swan picks up his Bible and moves towards June's desk. 'Miss Ayson, you always know where they are.'

'I'm sorry, Mr. Swan, I don't,' June is happy to tell him. 'And I wouldn't tell you if I did.'

'Then we'll find them together,' grits Swan. 'It's time we made an example of these slackers for Mr Clarke.'

He drags the surprised June toward the fire escape stairs.

Meera and Ben call the lift – none of the lifts have a thirtieth floor marked, but apparently they do come up here. They look up at one of the giant hissing ventilator grilles, working right above their heads. Ben studies it suspiciously. 'We shouldn't be breathing this. Let me know if you start to go nuts.'

The elevator doors open before them just as a group of directors turns into the corridor.

In the reception area, the pounding video screens are showing the kind of relentless, upbeat visuals that would drive anyone mad. Unable to take it any longer, Ms Thompson attempts to switch them off.

When she is unable to do this, she tries to tear the plugs from the wall, but they won't come out. In desperation, she drags the monitors down from their mounts by clambering onto them, sending them to the floor, where they explode in crackling rainbows of pixel light.

Miranda can't catch her breath. There is no more air left in the shaft. She hammers weakly on the walls. She feels her stomach lighten, and suddenly throws up.

Motorcycle couriers don't think about too much when they deliver packages. This one is whistling cheerfully to himself as he dismounts and strides inside the SymaxCorp building. Glad to get out of the rain, he crosses the lobby and is directed to the twentieth floor receptionist.

As soon as the lift doors open, he knows there's a problem. The air is thick, smouldering with soot and pieces of burning paper. Ms Thompson is seated at her granite desk, surrounded by small but fierce fires.

'I got a package for the marketing department,' he tells her. Ms Thompson carefully sets the package down in front of her. Something explodes on the wall behind them. He tries to ignore the problem. 'I need a signature. If you would initial …'

He gives the receptionist his signature pad and a pen. She

snaps the pen in half and throws it over her shoulder, then stares at him as if she is going to kill him.

'Sign underneath ...' he suggests.

She squirts lighter fuel over the pad and sets fire to it.

'... And, er, print your name. Or perhaps I'll just go. It's not a good time, is it? I'll just go, eh.'

The courier turns and walks away fast, trying to get the hell out, but the receptionist beats him to it. As Ms Thompson stares at this man in leathers who dares to pester her with demands, her eyes cloud liverishly. She brings him down with the kind of extraordinary flying tackle that Clarke wishes his son might one day make, and for good measure twists the poor boy's head back to front inside his crash helmet.

'All helmets must be removed!' she screams shrilly, before returning to her desk and collapsing onto it with a skull-fracturing thud.

Meera and Ben are descending through the building. The electricity powers down and the lights flicker as the elevator comes to a slow, grinding halt between floors.

'Now what?' asks Ben.

There is a metallic bang, and the elevator is plunged into darkness.

Swan has always had the capacity to become evangelical, but this is going too far. He has grabbed June's hands and is pulling her before him, pawing her in a distinctly un-Christian manner.

'Mr Swan,' yells June, 'you're hurting me!'

'Accept Jesus as your saviour,' commands Swan. 'We'll pray to the Lord together.'

June is horrified. 'But I'm an agnostic!'

'Then we must pray for your soul! Oh June, ever since I first saw you, I longed for the touch of your silken skin.' Swan falls on his knees in front of her, burying his head between her thighs.

Much to June's own surprise, she kicks him as hard as she can in the groin, feeling his pods retreat into his pelvic cavity.

Revolted, she hurries away from Swan, but he staggers to his feet and comes after her, seizing her arm. Most men would be rolling around on the floor for a while.

June breaks free and runs for the stairs, but Swan throws himself after her with abandon, and the pair crash to the edge of the landing. June is knocked cold. Swan has shattered a kneecap on the concrete steps, but this doesn't stop him from dragging her away. His eyes are clouded over with thick, white cataracts.

'*Vengeance is mine*, sayeth the Lord.' He feels the power of the Holy Spirit building within him, hears the swish of blood in his ears as germs invade his soft, pink brain.

Fitch looks up from her screen to realise that she is the only one still working on her part of the floor, although on the far side of the room a woman sits typing in the nude. Two financial controllers are attempting to rape a girl from Accounts. A junior technician is pissing onto his computer keyboard and screaming abuse at it. The mail boy is masturbating into an Amazon box. If Dante's Inferno had fire officers and a pension plan, it would have been like this.

Fitch tries to make sense of what she sees. Finally she gives up and starts pulling bottles of liquor out of her drawer. She lines up five bottles of Scorpion Vodka and proceeds to down them, one after the other. The alcohol scorches her throat and numbs her head; it's a good feeling.

Ben reaches up and pushes back the elevator hatch, then clambers up onto the roof in the lift shaft. It's dark, but he can see the maintenance ladder clearly. He starts climbing up to the floor above. Reaching the doors, he tries to force them open, but they won't budge. Just then, he hears a banging noise coming from the side of the shaft. He listens, then calls out: 'Miranda! Where are you?'

A faint voice. 'In here!'

Ben tracks the noise to a large, aluminium grille. He searches the grille for a way to release it. 'I can't get you out. Wait a minute.'

Just then, the power comes back on and the lift starts moving up toward him. Ben sees a loop of electrical cable hanging down near the grille and grabs one end, threading it through the grille. He finishes knotting it with seconds to spare as the lift carries him up.

Ben is still holding the end of the cable, which runs quickly through his hands. He scrambles back down though the roof hatch of the lift to Meera, and ties the cable around himself. 'Meera!' he shouts, 'take it down! Take the lift down!'

Ben hangs tight to the cable end, hoping the lift will pull the grille off. The lift stops, then starts to descend. They pass the grille. The cable pulls tight. But it doesn't pull the grille free, because Ben's weight isn't enough. What it does is haul Ben up out of the lift through its roof hatch.

Meera has sent the lift all the way down. Now she is madly punching the buttons, trying to stop it.

Ben is suspended from the cable in the lift shaft as the elevator retreats away from him. Only the grille is holding him, but it's cheaply made, and starts to pull free. Inside, Miranda tries to kick it free with her foot. 'That's it,' she shouts, 'it's coming!'

'No! Miranda, no!' yells Ben.

She smashes at the grille, helping to loosen it. She can't see the consequences. The grille's rivets pop out and the whole thing bends outwards. Ben desperately tries to swing back and forth in the shaft, his feet searching for some kind of foothold. The lift is a long way below him now, heading for the bottom of the shaft.

The grille is almost off. Miranda gives it a last hard kick with both feet, and it breaks free. Still attached to the grille by the cable, Ben drops like a stone.

Suddenly Miranda sees what's happened and tries to grab the falling grille – but she's too late.

Meera is trapped in the lift as it starts its ascent. Something heavy slams onto the roof, as Ben falls back through the hatch onto the floor. The cable and the grille follow him in and nearly decapitate Meera.

Miranda is now halfway out of the ventilator shaft when she sees the lift coming back up, and is forced to duck back inside. But she has lost her grip, and finds herself hanging on to Felix's putrescent corpse, which is slipping out with her. Moments later they are both half-hanging out of the shaft, about to be sliced in two by the lift. As Miranda scrambles over it, Felix's corpse slides free beneath her. The ascending lift rends Felix in half – easily slicing through the bad meat – and leaves Miranda flat on the roof.

Miranda falls into the lift in a liquid shower of guts. She lands on Meera. Ben's knees are bleeding, Meera is badly bruised and Miranda smells awful, but at least they're all alive.

By now, the open-plan office has become a macabre parody of its depiction in the company brochure. Two female marketing managers have been stripped and tied together, and their hair set on fire. Undercurrents of sex and violence have risen to the surface like marsh gas as workers obey their darkest instincts. Staff are wiping files, shredding papers, mutilating themselves, arguing, attempting sex, pulling off ties and brassieres, tearing at their buttons, fighting and mauling each other.

Clarke slips out of his office. He calls the lift, but then, rather than wait, decides to take the stairs. He doesn't see that the lift doors have opened behind him, revealing the remains of Draycott's corpse and three people coated in decaying offal. He passes Swan, who is dragging the screaming June down the stairs behind him.

Ben and Meera help Miranda out of the lift. They slip and slide, heading for the ladies' toilets. Miranda will be the hardest to wash clean. 'He must have been there for weeks, just rotting to bits,' gasps Miranda.

Meera knows what happened now. 'The system is replacing the germs with stronger chemicals,' she says. 'It hasn't gone wrong. If anything, it's just being efficient. We've got to shut it down.'

'It'd be quicker to get everyone out of the building,' Ben tells them.

'Yeah? How are you going to do that?'

'There must be a fire alarm box somewhere.'

'The heat-sensors should have responded by now and turned the sprinklers on.'

'Then we have to tell the staff what's happening, and pull them out ourselves.'

They push open the doors to the open-plan office and find themselves in a Brueghelian nightmare of orgiastic chaos. The staff have put Meadows' stereo unit on; it's playing very loud trance music. The air is dense and dirty.

Miranda stands there with her hands on her hips. 'Do you want to tell them, or shall I?'

9. FRIDAY 1:49 PM

Faced with a full-scale staff riot, Meera and Ben are trying to think what to do. 'What about blocking the air ducts?' suggests Meera.

'There are hundreds all over the building.'

'Then we'll do it another way. Call the police.' Meera grabs the nearest phone and punches out a number. Ear-splitting feedback causes her to drop the receiver.

She tries her mobiles – all IT staff seem to have at least three – but the signal is scrambled. 'Now that is electro-magnetic interference. There's no way of getting through to the outside.'

'Try the computers.'

The same goes for the internet and e-mail systems. As Miranda logs on, the computer screens start rolling with static and weird images. An old episode of *Bewitched* seems to be playing on many of the terminals.

Ben sees that the directors' offices are empty. He calls out to one of his colleagues, Jake, who is busy feeding his hard-copy documents into a waste-bin fire.

'Where are the directors?' he asks.

'They're up with Dr Samphire, preparing for the satellite presentation on the top floor.'

'I can go downstairs and see if the lobby doors are still open,' Miranda offers. Doing something will make her feel better.

Sally, one of the office assistants, is lying across her desk, being licked and fondled by two work mates. 'Don't do it, Miranda,' she pleads. 'Some of us don't need the outside world anymore.' Her eyes are rolled over into the whites – no pupils at all. 'I'm sick of being told what to do every working day of my fucking life. Ask yourself what's better; invoicing or a really good orgasm?' One of her lickees takes Meera's mobiles away from her and smashes them. Sally laughs hysterically.

'It almost seems a shame to spoil the fun,' says Ben.

'Nevertheless, I think we'd better spoil it before someone else gets killed, don't you?' Meera snaps back. 'There are over a thousand people in this building, and right now, most of them are going insane.'

'We're not.'

'You've been here less than a week. Miranda temps, and I had a holiday. None of us has worked through the whole night. It's the ones who have had prolonged exposure that worry me.'

Miranda is prepared to set off alone. 'I can look after myself,' she tells them. 'I know my way around this place. I'll meet you back here. If I can get away, I'll call the police.' She kisses Ben. 'When we get out of this place, I'm going to show you how to relieve stress. Horizontally.'

10. FRIDAY 2:07 PM

Ben and Meera make their way up, but progress is slow, as burning pieces of furniture are being thrown down the centre of the stairwell. The air is acrid with smoke. The security guard who whacked him earlier rises from the steps in front of Ben. His eyes are white, too.

'Fucking hell, not you again,' Ben complains. The guard takes out his Taser and fires it up.

'This is going to hurt you more than it hurts me,' he promises. A blue arc cracks between the weapon's points. Behind him, Meera detaches a fire extinguisher from the wall and brings it down hard on the guard's head.

'I wouldn't bet on it.' Meera would like to take the extinguisher with her, but it's too heavy. She's hitched up her sari to an undignified, but rather fetching, height.

Ben pockets the guard's Taser. Incredibly, the guard gets to his feet behind their backs and comes after them again. Ben swings around the stair-pole and kicks him hard in the face. The guard goes down –

– and gets back up.

Ben wonders what they're feeding him. The guard grabs Meera around the neck and starts choking her. Ben remembers the Taser and powers it into the guard's groin. The guard screams and collapses –

– and gets back up.

'He's got balls.' Meera and Ben nod to each other, then drop to the guard's legs and tip him over the stairwell. This time he hits his head on every landing, spinning madly. He won't be coming back again. They continue upwards.

'I'll do the directors,' Ben suggests, 'you do Room 3014.'

'Got it.' They split up when they hit the top floor.

11. FRIDAY 2:16 PM

Meera runs to Room 3014 and uses Clarke's key to open the door. Inside, she goes to the air-con system's master control box and tries to open it. She gets the razor-sharp doors apart, but is dumbfounded by the maze of electronics before her. She doesn't see Clarke coming up behind her, raising his cricket bat. The bat has steel edges that look as if they've been sharpened for some purpose other than hitting sixes.

'You disappoint me, Miss Mangeshkar,' says the supervisor. 'A bright girl like you stepping out of line, tampering with company property, jeopardising your career advancement.'

Ignoring him, Meera turns on the Taser. She applies it to the machinery, causing a small explosion that shorts out the system. But, as she watches, the system's electronics neatly reroute themselves.

'That'll be the tamper-proof protection system. I've been watching you for a while, Miss Mangeshkar. Your spelling is atrocious.' Clarke slowly lowers the cricket bat. Instead, he snatches the Taser from Meera and hits her in the stomach with it. Meera convulses in shock.

'As a consequence of your inattention to detail, your employment here is officially terminated.' Clarke hits her with the Taser again. Another violent shock.

'Kindly empty your desk and see the human resources officer.' He hits her with the Taser a third time.

'A suitable reference will be forwarded to you.'

Meera's body is wracked by electrical activity, and she collapses, almost losing consciousness. Clarke lifts his raised boot and swings a vicious kick at her. 'We hope your time with us has been enjoyable and instructive,' he concludes.

Meera rallies for a last-ditch attempt at stopping the man who employed her. She rises painfully to her feet with arms raised, ready to put her kickboxing lessons into practice, but she's small and slender, while Clarke is heavy-set and demented. The supervisor's eyes slowly cloud over, the pupils simply fading away. Meera sees the change and flinches, preparing for the worst …

… as Clarke again raises his cricket bat.

12. FRIDAY 2:25 PM

Miranda has had a tough time getting downstairs. The lobby is in chaos as she reaches it. The main doors to the building are locked. She tries them all – same story. She runs to the dazed reception guard. 'Is there a way of opening these manually?' she asks.

The guard is catatonic, motionless. 'I went to university,' he tells her.

'I'm sorry?'

'I have a master's degree in art history. Just so that I could wind up as a fucking security guard. A fucking trained Alsatian could do this job. A blind one. With three legs.'

'The key. I need the door key.'

'My mother didn't raise me to stand watch over some rich fucker's property.'

'The key!' she shouts, slapping his face hard and preparing to duck in case he hits her back. But it seems to do the trick.

'There's a single master that overrides all the deadbolts to the outer doors and the atrium.'

'Where is it?'

'Out there.' The guard points through the glass to the foliage-covered annexe.

The white-eyed Swan is just finishing locking the door to the atrium from the inside. He pockets the special deadbolt key and continues to pull June behind him. Although she is now conscious again, he has tied her hands together. He drags her across the forest floor of the atrium. 'You'll get what's coming to you, you painted Jezebel,' he pants. 'My God, you could afford to lose some weight.'

Meera is small, but she's fast. As Clarke swings his bat, she drops to her knees and grabs his raised boot, tipping him off-balance. Clarke is back on his feet in moments. Obsessive men have hidden reserves of power. Roaring like a bear, he slams Meera backward into one of the floor-to-ceiling panes of glass, with tremendous force. The glass holds, but its surround doesn't. The whole thing starts to crack around the edges. Clarke charges forward, pinning Meera against the glass with his orthopaedic boot as the rest of the frame cracks.

Clarke shakes his head piteously. 'If only you could have learned to wear a dress like the other girls.' He pushes down hard.

The entire panel divorces itself from the frame and falls out, taking Meera with it.

She falls slowly at first, almost gracefully. Meera plummets through space, sailing down on the glass sheet.

As Swan manhandles June on her stomach across the atrium, June hears a strange noise – shattering glass – and looks up. Swan looks up, too. The sheet of glass carrying Meera explodes through the roof of the atrium. Non-lethal fragments rain down, but the great window pane lands on Swan, shearing him in half at the softest point of his waist, and spraying June in blood.

Meera falls through the roof into the top of a tall, artificial palm tree.

From inside the building, Miranda hammers on the doors. June looks up at her in a daze. 'June!' she shouts, 'June! You have to get the key!' But June is too stunned to register anything. 'The key! In his pocket! The key!'

As June gathers her senses, she realises what Miranda is asking of her. She reaches into the still-twitching corpse's jacket and fishes for the key. As she does so, the top half of Swan convulses violently, making her scream. The half-a-corpse latches onto her, pulling her over and trying to drag itself on top. The ragged stump of Swan's spinal cord is poking out from the bottom of his rib cage, so June stamps on it. As Swan falls back with a gurgling yell, she grabs the key and makes for the entrance door.

She has trouble finding the lock, but spots it and inserts the key. While she's trying to twist it, Half-Swan starts clawing at her. Oddly, his lower half appears to have died. It's only the part with the brain in that she has to worry about now. His right hand is trying to lock itself around her ankle. This is definitely sexual harassment, as defined in the office bible.

13. FRIDAY 2:37 PM

Ben reaches the directors' boardroom and bursts in.

The directors number a dozen men, no women – there's a surprise. They are seated beside Dr Hugo Samphire, drinking coffee at the long, walnut-veneer table, which is surrounded by colour-coded plans on raised boards. Some are furtively eating digestive biscuits. The front-man is talking to his New York audience at the start of the satellite video presentation. They're completely oblivious to what's been going on below.

'Who are you?' Dr Samphire snaps at Ben. 'The satellite presentation is about to start. What the hell do you mean by barging your way in here?'

Ben is momentarily dumbfounded. He looks at the wall vents, which should be pumping the same poisoned air into the room as in the rest of the building. 'You give your staff different air,' he says, amazed that Miranda has been right all along.

The directors are glancing at each other; how can an employee know about this? The audience on the video monitor is starting to look puzzled.

'Kill the link,' someone orders. 'We'll call them back.' One of the directors breaks the satellite connection. 'You have to leave right now. Somebody call security.'

Ben is starting to understand the true nature of management. 'You don't even know what's going on down there, do you?' he realises. One of the directors is trying to call security, but having no luck. 'The line's dead,' he tells the others.

Dr Samphire's sense of order has been affronted. 'There's nothing in the air that's not perfectly safe to breathe,' he bridles.

'There's a dead body in the main ventilation shaft.'

'You're lying.'

'Think so? Try breathing this.' Ben goes to the door and slams it wide open. On the other side of the corridor, he wedges open the stairwell door. The poisonous air pours in, rolling across the floor like plague-pit fumes.

'The compounds we're using will all be fully approved.'

'You added drugs.'

'Only to enhance efficiency for the purpose of preparing today's presentation.' Dr Samphire tries to sound reasonable in a we're-all-men-of-the-world way.

'Meanwhile, just to be on the safe side, you had a separate air supply installed up here.'

'We don't need to work as hard as our staff. We're directors.'

The directors are in an uproar. Nobody wants to risk breathing the bad air. They are arguing among themselves, two or three heading for Ben, when Clarke appears in the stairwell doorway. He has his razor-edged cricket bat slung across his back like some kind of Home Counties bounty hunter.

'Mr Harper reports to me,' Clarke explains. 'I'll enjoy taking care of this.'

With the door between June and Miranda, June fights to get the deadbolt key in the bottom lock. Half-Swan appears to have vanished into the tropical undergrowth, wriggling away like some kind of grotesque reptile. Meera chooses this moment to fall out of the tree, hanging onto the palm fronds, and lands in the soft earth. With her sari torn open, Meera increasingly looks like a Bollywood action heroine, except when she opens her mouth.

'Jesus Fuck. Ow. Bollocks.'

June is shouting for someone to help her. Meera grabs the key and turns it, opening the door. As she does so, and pulls herself and June through, Half-Swan springs from the bushes, hauling himself along by his hands, shoving his way inside with them. He slams the door shut, turns the key in the lock and makes off with it, dragging himself away into darkness.

'Christ, what is keeping him alive?' asks the shocked Miranda. She turns to June, who has fallen in beside her. 'There's got to be another way out.' She looks at the torn and bleeding Meera. 'What the hell happened to you?'

'I fell out of the building, all right? We need to find Howard.'

'Why?'

'Let's just find him, okay?'

Clarke walks Ben ahead of him, goading him with the razor-sharp tip of his cricket bat. 'This is what happens when you leave your workstation unattended.'

'Have you seen what's going on down there?'

'What's the matter, Mr Harper, are you afraid of a little hard work?'

'It's not the work that bothers me, it's the mass psychosis of a building filled with deranged, homicidal maniacs.'

'That's the trouble with people like you, Harper. There's always an excuse.' He swings the bat at Ben's throat, and somehow manages to pin him to the railings by the handle. He produces a huge roll of silver tape and starts taping Ben up.

'You killed Felix,' says Ben, dumbly.

'A little man trying to hold back a big industry. People like him – people like you – don't deserve to survive. I bet you don't even vote.'

'Why did you hide his body in the air-pipe?'

'To infect the others.' Met with an uncomprehending stare, he sighs and explains. 'From the day I started work, I just wanted to do my job well. After thirty years of late nights and no holidays, I became a supervisor. I had no friends, no woman, no life, but it didn't matter. I sacrificed everything for my employers. Then along came Mr Draycott …'

… Clarke studied Draycott, hating his crisp, white shirt and gym-toned chest, hating the cool, young new boy with all the answers in his report. He raised his cricket bat, and his righteous anger did the rest.

Disposing of the body was a bit of a fag, though. He had to drag, shove, fold, drop and bend Draycott to get him inside the grille, ramming him through to the steel shaft below. As the body landed with a slam, his employment papers drifted down after him. Moments later, the air-con system started up. That, of course, was the problem right there …

'Don't you think I knew my days were numbered?' Clarke hisses at him. 'All I ever wanted was a little respect. A little acknowledgement. Was that too much to ask?'

Now completely taped up, Ben is stuck at the top of the stairwell. The worst thing is having to listen to his supervisor play the sympathy card. 'I can see how you feel,' he says carefully. 'If you don't have a job in this country, people treat you like shit.'

'They treat you like shit if you do,' warns Clarke, somewhat mollified. 'When I come back, I'm afraid I'm going to have to terminate your contract.'

14. FRIDAY 3:05 PM

June, Meera and Miranda are keeping an eye out for Half-Swan, who has scuttled off again. They round a corner in the basement and find Howard in his deckchair, smoking dope and listening to the Chemical Brothers on his iPod. He smiles and peace-signs them.

'Hey guys.' Howard wants to high-five, but nobody's in the mood. Half-Swan is sitting on top of a tool cabinet above him, poised to drop and attack. His colon is hanging below his shirt-tails.

Meera yanks Howard's headphones off, pulling him backwards. She and Miranda drag Howard clear into the next room as Swan throws himself at the flimsy door, hammering it hard.

'Don't you know what's happening up there?' asks Meera.

'Holy Jesus Mother Of God! What the fuck was that?'

'Mr Swan,' says June. 'The top half of him, anyway. He's kind of dead but he won't lie down.'

'No shit. Oh man, I warned you. No pain receptors, your brain keeps functioning as long as they tell your heart to keep beating. I fucking *knew* this would happen.'

'How did you know?' asks Miranda.

'Oh fuck.' Howard looks sheepish. 'You're looking for someone to blame, it's me. I designed the SymaxCorp system.'

'You?'

'Yeah. I started when I was still at school – didn't come out of my room for about three years. It was all theory, of course. Dr

81

Samphire found me and made it happen. I ran it through every conceivable scenario, then pointed out the potential problems. He had some ideas of his own about those. He wanted to keep me where he could keep an eye on me. One of his little jokes; the whizz kid becoming the janitor. I don't mind it down here. It's cosy.'

'I thought the directors were to blame,' says Miranda, disillusioned.

'Yeah, right. Most of them couldn't find their own dicks with a microscope and tweezers. A profound lack of imagination is the only quality you need to rule the fucking world.'

Half-Swan slams himself at the plywood door, nearly breaking through.

'How's he kicking the door without any legs?' June wonders.

Miranda looks around. 'Is there another way out of here apart from the front doors?'

'This isn't like one of those *Alien* films where they keep pulling out maps of service pipes. Duh.' Howard rolls his eyes.

'Come on Howard, there must be something!'

'Well obviously there's a rubbish chute, but you can only get to it from the atrium, 'cause that's where they take the recycling stuff.'

'We can get there.'

'The tunnel's full of rubbish.'

'We can clear it.'

'And it's welded shut.'

'I thought you designed all this?' Miranda accuses.

'Don't rush me,' says Howard. 'Somebody roll a joint while I'm thinking,'

Ben comes to. He's tied to a wheeled desk chair with rolls of parcel tape. His mouth is taped. Perhaps Clarke wants to keep him alive as a sympathetic ear? He tries to move the chair, but it's at the top of the stairwell flight, and one false move will send him to his death.

There's a loose end to the tape. There's also a trolley ramp on

82

the first flight of stairs. Ben manages to fix the tape around the stair-rail with one hand. He kicks back. The chair tips down the stairs, spinning on its stem as the tape unravels. But it rolls too fast, shooting off the edge of the staircase and over into the stairwell. The tape pulls tight as he falls.

Ben and chair are yanked back, to hang suspended in space by the attached tape.

Miranda, Meera, June and Howard back away from the door, which is being violently battered and is splitting in half.

Howard points ahead. 'There's a cable tunnel that goes as far as the lobby, but it's not very wide.' He eyes June as he speaks. 'I don't know if she'll go through.'

'At least try – we'll deal with the supervisor.' Miranda looks like she's been waiting for something like this all her working career.

'If you guys are sure,' says Howard, uncertainly.

'He hasn't got any bloody legs, Howard, all right? We can manage.'

Howard can't wait to get out. He takes June with him. As Miranda and Meera barricade the breaking door, a dark shape shifts behind them. They turn around to find Miss Fitch in an alcove, chopping up documents on an old-fashioned paper-guillotine. She must have been there the whole time. She's smoking hard and slugging vodka from the bottle.

'I have so much paperwork, you have no idea.' Her eyes are as white as the paper she slices. 'It's my job to make the directors look good. I've been rewriting their mail and remembering their wives' birthdays for six fucking years on a bare living wage, and what thanks do I get?' She slams down the guillotine blade. '*What thanks do I get?*' She shouts so hard that everyone jumps.

Fitch looks down. She has cut her wrist through to the bone. The severed artery is spraying blood everywhere. 'Oh, *for Heaven's sake*. I just had a manicure.' She attempts to carry on working, her wrist flapping, pumping blood all around as Miranda looks on in horror.

Just then, Half-Swan breaks in and recognises Miss Fitch. He halts before her. She's bleeding really badly. His guts are falling out. They're not a great couple.

'I'm a woman with feelings,' Fitch continues, oblivious. 'I have desires and needs. Nobody notices. It took you six years to ask me out on a date, Mr Swan. You spent the whole evening talking about work, then left me outside a kebab shop. I've had better nights.'

'You've seen better days.'

'This? It's just a paper cut. Where are your legs?'

Swan looks down in some surprise. 'What – ? Where's the rest of me?'

'There's some of you in the atrium,' Miranda tells him. 'You are *so* past your sell-by date, Swan.'

Swan sighs. 'This is where equal opportunities gets you. Women in business are such *bitches*.' He makes a sudden move to strangle Fitch. Miranda spots the deadbolt key sticking out of Swan's pocket and snatches it away. She grabs Meera and they get the hell out.

They run along the cable tunnel, emerging into the lobby, where sex and anarchy rule. It's a scene from the uncut version of *Caligula*. The few members of staff who haven't gone insane are hammering at the glass doors, trying to get out. Miranda and Meera attempt to walk through them with a little dignity. Meera tears off the lower half of her sari, which keeps catching on stuff.

They approach the doors with the deadbolt key. But just as Miranda is about to use it, a huge creature lumbers from the shadows and snatches it from her.

It is Clarke, armed with his razor-bat, his combover sticking up at a fantastic angle. Miranda screams.

'Jameson,' he hisses. 'Our little company rebel. And Miss Indiana Fucking Jones. I thought I threw you out of the building.' Miranda can see he has the key – their only means of escape.

'What have you done with Ben?' she asks, making a grab for the key. He holds it high above her, teasing. Then he opens his mouth and drops it in.

'He's swallowed it,' says Miranda, 'Meera, he's swallowed it!'

15. FRIDAY 3:23 PM

Upstairs, the directors are in chaos. Some have handkerchiefs over their faces, and all are trying to get out. Two are heading for the SymaxCorp system mainframe, hoping to dismantle it somehow.

Dr Samphire looks frustrated. It's not an emotion he's used to. 'There must be some way we can shut it down.'

'You'd have to override the building's entire power supply,' one of the other directors explains.

'Well whose brilliant fucking idea was that?'

The director smirks mirthlessly. 'That would be yours, sir.'

Miranda struggles up the stairs after Meera. Clarke is locked around Miranda's waist, dragging himself behind her like a human anchor. Remembering that she is still wearing her fashionably-pointed shoes, she twists and jams one into Clarke's gullet. Gagging, he falls away.

Miranda sees Ben hanging over the stairwell, and runs up until she's level with his head, ripping off his mouth tape. Then she hauls him toward her. As she's doing so, Clarke makes a fresh grab for her, who is forced to let go of Ben's chair.

The chair swings dangerously out across the stairwell. Miranda tries to fight off Clarke as Ben's tape starts to break. Meera tries to grab at the swinging chair, but misses it.

Miranda gives as good as she gets, slamming Clarke against the stairwell wall. Clarke is feeling no pain, only rage. He grabs Miranda by the throat and lifts her from the ground, choking the life from her. Ben is helpless to save her. Meera is still trying to haul him in.

Miranda is close to blacking out as Clarke's fat fingers dig in. Ben kicks out hard, swinging the chair on its tape-rope. On his third swing, he slams into Clarke, knocking him back against the wall.

The tape breaks. Meera makes a flying save and grabs the back of Ben's chair, but it almost pulls her over the railing. Clarke breaks free and uses the confusion to head off up the stairs.

'Miranda!' yells Meera. 'I can't hold it!' Miranda grabs Ben just as he tears loose from the chair and Meera lets the chair go. It tumbles down into the stairwell with a clatter. Together, they pull the tape off Ben.

Ben rubs his sore mouth. 'Where did Clarke go?'

'Up. He swallowed the door-key.'

They run after him.

Clarke is on the floor above them.

The supervisor reaches Room 3014, and the empty window frame where Meera nearly fell to her death. Meera, Ben and Miranda are close behind, but they shoot past him in the shadowy corridors.

'Where's he gone?' Meera turns. They all turn and look.

As they pass the glass wall at the end of the corridor, Ben sees the empty window-cleaning cradle outside.

'That's our way out of the building. Who wants to do this?'

Meera waves the idea off like a bad smell. 'Forget it. I've already been outside the hard way.'

Ben finds a slim door in the wall, opens it and climbs out. He has to walk along a ledge to reach the cradle. Up here, the wind is blowing so hard that the rain is travelling sideways.

'See if you can get anyone down to the lobby,' he shouts. 'I'll meet you there from the other side, I hope.' Ben eyes the cradle uncomfortably. He tries to operate the electric panel that works the cradle, which at least is on steel runners down the side of the building, not ropes. He has no idea how to operate it, but gamely takes off the brake.

The steel cage plunges like a roller coaster. For a moment, Ben is freefalling above it, clinging to the handrail, before he can pull himself down to slam the brake back on. The cradle slows and stops. It had dropped one floor. Ben eases off on the brake and the cradle starts to slide slowly down the building, cutting a swathe through the wind and driving rain.

One more floor and the cage suddenly jams and stops at an angle, jarring Ben to the grid floor. Far below him spin giant ventilator blades, sucking fresh air into the building for processing. He slithers to the edge of the tilted cradle, catching the ledge of the building with his outstretched hands.

At that moment, Clarke slams up against the fire escape windows beside Ben, grinning maniacally. For a man with a built-up boot, he has a way of moving damned fast when he wants something. He examines the window for a moment, testing for its weak point, then swings his bat and splinters the glass, which crazes but holds. He pulls the bat free and swings again.

This time the tip gets through, in a shower of crystalline fragments.

The cradle tilts further and Ben is left hanging on the outside of the building.

Clarke reaches through and slams down the bat – but Ben moves his hands before he can connect. The supervisor climbs on board the cradle, his blade spraying a shower of sparks as it connects with the steel braking mechanism.

The cradle unfreezes and races straight down the building, with Ben and Clarke hanging on for their lives. Moments from the bottom, the automatic safety system is triggered and slams in, slowing the cradle abruptly and flattening Ben and Clarke on its floor. As Ben rises to scramble out, Clarke brains him with the butt of the bat, knocking him into semi-consciousness.

Clarke hits the cradle's up button, sending it skyward and knocking Ben off balance. They fight for the controls. Clarke grips his bat handle and prepares to swing for England. This should be good enough to finish the match.

'Your innings is over,' he warns, kicking Ben back with his

orthopaedic boot. As the cradle continues its rapid ascent, he starts to push Ben over the side with the sharp edge of the bat. Ben feels a hot line of blood forming through his wet shirt. Pinned like this, unable to move, he knows he is about to die.

He sees Clarke's raised boot coming at him and grabs it, twisting hard. Clarke screams as Ben lifts it – and him – over and out of the cradle. Leverage always wins over brute strength.

Clarke falls and slams onto the ventilator grating, where he lies stuck above the sucking fans. Ben watches as the lightweight aluminium safety bars slowly bend apart beneath his weight. Mr Clarke, senior supervisor, thirty years of faithful service in the private finance sector, is sucked into the grating, exploding as he hits the first of the fans. The supervisor's remains hurtle around and up the ventilation shaft to his final destination.

The last of Clarke comes out of the steel rooftop chimney in a spectacular crimson fountain.

Miranda and Meera see Clarke's minced innards rain down on the outside of the building. As the pulverised remains fall, something shiny and metallic passes them and bounces onto the roof of the atrium below.

'Jesus,' Miranda exclaims, 'the key!' She and Meera rush back to the stairwell. 'There must be a service door onto the atrium roof.'

Ben is hanging onto the rising, still-tipped cradle. He looks up. If he doesn't stop it, he'll hit the top at incredible speed. He looks for the controls but finds only bare wires. It would appear that Clarke took the hand control panel with him when he fell. Ben can do nothing but wait to be flung from the cradle in the final crash.

Unless.

He sees, coming up, the broken window from which Clarke emerged. He is ascending at an incredible speed. He'll have just one shot.

The gaping hole shoots past his feet. Ben lets go of the side of the tipped cradle and slides in through the window, just as he passes it.

16. FRIDAY 4:05PM

Meera and Miranda find Ben lying in the stairwell on the twenty eighth floor. It takes a minute to get him awake, but they succeed in pulling him to his feet.

'We have to shut the systems down,' he says.

'Wait,' says Miranda. 'That means shutting everything down. Power. Lights. Air. The place will be sealed tight. You want to turn it into a big steel coffin full of raving maniacs?'

Meera shrugs. 'It works for me.'

They head back to the top floor and room 3014. Miranda opens the master control panel and looks around for some way of disarming it. 'This needs the female touch,' she warns, smashing a steel chair into the system, which makes no difference at all. Meera stops her and follows the cabling to a DANGER: LIVE VOLTAGE box. She unclips the lid, overrides the protector panel and removes a water cooler tank, emptying the whole lot into the mains.

There are several small explosions and a lot of sparks, but the air system reroutes again and remains on, its gauges moving even further into overcompensation. Throughout the building, floor by floor, the lights go out and the windows darken.

Miranda stands up and brushes herself down. 'Nice one,' she says, sarcastically. 'Terrific. This top was brand new. We can't stop it. Now what do we do?'

'Get the key back. Get the hell out.'

Meera heads off after the key.

17. FRIDAY 4:17PM

The directors watch as the mainframe diverts itself to keep running. They are panicked and still trying not to inhale the atmosphere, although it's hopeless pretending you won't breathe. 'There must be some way to turn the damned air off,' Dr Samphire insists.

'Ultimately, it's designed to reroute itself to an outside power supply if there's a crisis. It can't be turned off.' This from the same smartarse director who was rude to him before. When this is over …

'What you're telling me is we're fucked. That boy. He knew what was wrong. You have to find him.'

The other director looks disgusted. *What happened to 'we'?* he wonders.

The work-floor is a very different place now. The air is as thick and as murky as the bottom of a pond. The windows have automatically darkened, screening out the light. In the hazy beam of Miranda's torch, lunatics flit past in various states of undress. The building is a heathen hell, where small fires burn on desks. The few remaining computers are smashed in. Some of the sprinklers are on. There are moans and screams in the dark. Bedlam was an oasis of sanity by comparison.

Ben is still suffering from the effects of his fall. Miranda searches for survivors. Hearing a whimpering sound from under one of the desks, she finds a battered but still-living friend.

'June?' She helps her out from the crawlspace. 'Are you okay?'

'I think so.'

They are heading for the stairwell door when Miss Fitch reappears in front of them, lurching out of the semi-gloom. Her hair is standing on end. She's trailing a computer keyboard, and has sellotape stuck all over her, with scissors, pens, and other bits of office equipment hanging from her body. Her cut wrist flops uselessly. She's covered in coagulating blood.

'Where do you two think you're going? Have you finished all your work?'

'There's no more work to do. It's over.'

Fitch, with her good hand, plucks some fluff from her sweater in annoyance. 'You know, ever since you came here, there's been disruption and insubordination. All this is your fault. If you hadn't started trying to upset the status quo, we wouldn't be trapped in here now.'

June taps Miranda on the shoulder. Miranda turns around. The deranged staff from her floor are standing behind Fitch in a semi-circle, watching the pair of them. The weaker ones always wait for a leader to emerge. It pays to be on the winning side.

Fitch works the crowd. 'You see what she's done? She's destroyed your careers! Why isn't *she* affected? You can't let her get away with this!'

The crowd surges forward, backing Miranda and June against the stairwell doors. The girls slip through, dragging Ben with them, jamming the handles shut on the other side with a chair leg – but it won't hold for long.

Miranda, Ben and June intend to head down the stairs, but another group of Bedlamites, this one in the mob colours now adopted by the accountancy floor, are on the way up.

The trio are forced to go up, not down. They hear the noise of the angry mob below them. The doors are smashed apart with fire-axes. Miranda grabs the partially-comatose Ben and smacks him hard in the face, causing him to revive a little. They are forced to continue upwards as the doors below burst open, and the Workforce of the Living Dead attack.

Have you ever been in an office where there's a hostile environment? Now imagine that times a million. And give them all weapons.

The angry lynch-mob, led by Fitch, Half-Swan and the remaining supervisors, move fast. Ben, June and Miranda whack them back, knocking them down only to see them rise again. They're only just managing to stay ahead. Somehow they reach the directors' floor and get inside, barricading the stairwell doors behind them. Two of the directors are still there.

'If you've got any bright ideas about how to get out of here, now's the time to suggest them,' says Miranda. The directors look helplessly at one another. *So much for executive decisions.* Miranda checks Ben's eyes. They're clouding over. Didn't he once have a nervous breakdown? She doesn't like the look of him. He needs to be taken outside into the fresh air, fast.

'What's above us?' asks June.

One of the directors looks at her as if she's mad. 'The roof, you stupid bitch. There's no way down from there.'

'Even if we could get back down,' June tells Miranda, 'we still don't have the door key.'

'Then we have to make our stand here.'

18. FRIDAY 4:28PM

As they speak, Meera has located the service door and is stepping out onto the glass roof of the atrium, which is still slippery with pieces of shredded Clarke. The key is lying on a vast, unsupported pane of cracked glass. As Meera ventures towards it, the pane starts to splinter like ice on a lake. *This isn't in my job description*, she thinks, dropping flat on the glass and starting to inch her way across it. The key seems miles away.

Upstairs, the last stand is taking place.

June, Ben and Miranda are as prepared as they'll ever be. The two directors are sheltering behind them. 'They're coming through,' yells June. As the remaining barrier between the sane and the insane starts to splinter, Miranda turns on the two cowering directors. 'We should just throw you out there to die.'

'Don't do that! I'm in a position to grant promotion,' promises some gormless-looking guy in a grey Burtons suit. 'I'm a very powerful man!'

Miranda looks at his groin. 'I think you've pissed yourself,' she points out.

The other director tries to reason. 'They're our employees. They'll listen to us. They'll still recognise the voice of a superior, surely?'

His colleague opens the door to get out. 'Surely? Fuck you, college boy, I'm out of here!' Then, too late, he realises what he's done.

The mob is through the doors now and pouring in, a screaming mass of blank-eyed workforce insanity. Ben tries to help the directors, but it's too late. The angry horde pours in around the shattered door, falling on the two men. They set about tearing their bosses limb from limb.

'Stop!' shout the directors. 'Think of your careers! You'll never work in this town again! We're in a position to grant you substantial financial awards!' But they still die horribly. By the time their attackers have finished, the room looks like an abattoir. Ben, Miranda and June are forced to run again.

There's an extremely stylish Colefax & Fowler executive bathroom at the end of the corridor. The trio barricade themselves inside.

'Now what do we do?' asks Ben.

'I don't know. The doors won't hold long.' Miranda senses someone behind her. She slowly turns. 'June –'

The white-eyed June jumps onto her back with a furious scream. Ben slams them both back into the wall behind, knocking June off-balance, but she's back on her feet in seconds and fighting viciously. She hurls Miranda aside and attacks Ben.

June cracks Ben's head against the sink – again – again. Water from the taps is spraying everywhere. Ben kicks June's feet out from under her. She slips on the wet floor and is impaled by the roof of her mouth on one of the taps. Red water pumps from her lips.

'Jesus – June –' Ben fearfully examines June's eyes. 'It's some final stage of poisoning.'

'The air – the ventilation shaft goes all the way down, doesn't it?' Miranda looks up at the wall ventilation unit. Ben climbs up onto a sink and starts hammering at the grille, but it's sealed shut. He desperately looks around the bathroom. As the shouts outside get louder, he grabs one of the heavy cistern lids and starts slamming it into the grille.

It bursts open just as the bathroom door starts coming apart. He pushes Miranda up, and then climbs in after her.

They start along the wide pipe, which meets up with the main ventilator shaft – a sheer vertiginous drop of hundreds of feet. The only way down is via a thin steel maintenance ladder. Above, they can hear the nightmarish sounds of the invading workers.

Miranda stops dead. 'I can't do it, Ben, not again. I've got no strength left.'

'You have to,' he says simply. He attempts to carry her, but she's awkward and nervous. He slips and falls. They land on the outcrop of another shaft twelve feet down.

He doggedly picks her up, but finds he's damaged his leg badly. Above them, the first of the crazed workers – could it be Mr Beamish from Costings and Estimates? – arrives through the pipe and plunges past them into the shaft. As he falls, he makes a grab for Miranda and very nearly pulls her in with him, but Ben hangs onto her for dear life. She leads the way down – but the section of ladder suddenly ends. It's a distance of at least twenty feet to where the next section starts.

'That's it,' says Ben, 'We're screwed.'

'At least we were going down this time.'

There's a tunnel opening to their left. It's a swing and a drop, but now they're beyond caring for their own safety. Ben kicks out the grating at the end of it.

They land in the corridor of the deserted ninth floor, and head toward the stairwell. Ben can barely walk. Somewhere above them are eerie booms and screams, all manner of mayhem.

At least the coast looks clear. They continue their descent through smoke, past smaller fires. Shadowy figures dash past ahead. They are in still in the realm of nightmares. Eight floors, one after the other. There's hardly anyone left alive, and certainly no-one sane.

On the ground floor of the stairwell, someone emerges very slowly and silently from the shadows. His face is blackened with ash, and his wide eyes are a hard, dead white. He learned stealth from an early age. There's nothing like inherited wealth for instilling guile. A huge hunting rifle is beside him, an extension of his arm.

Dr Samphire might not realise it, but he's showing how he earned his nickname of Dracula.

Ben and Miranda hobble down the stairs. Above them, crazies are starting to spill into the stairwell. The frenzied staffers are gaining on them. In great pain, Ben drags himself on, with Miranda trying to speed him up.

'We won't be able to get out at the bottom,' he shouts.

'What the fuck else can we do?' she yells. 'You want to stay up there and die?'

They reach the staircase above the ground floor of the stairwell. Dr Samphire slinks back into the shadows, watching and waiting for his moment.

They start running through the darkened ground floor. Ahead, its doors wide open, is the great glass atrium with its tropical forest of real and fake plants.

They look up and are amazed to see that the key is still there on the atrium roof. A few feet away from it is Meera, stranded on crazed patterns of cracked glass. She's almost there, but can go no further.

As Ben and Miranda run into the atrium, Dr Samphire steps from between the lurid artificial palm trees, the rifle across his chest. He's making a last stand in the business jungle.

They can't go forward – and, thanks to the angry mob pouring into the ground floor behind them, they can't go back.

'Well, well.' Dr Samphire doesn't look at all happy with them. 'Disruption, chaos, anarchy, disorder. Another great temple of commerce brought to its knees by people who don't know the meaning of an honest day's work. I hope you're very pleased with yourselves.' He walks toward them calmly, raising the rifle high. *Think of them as deer*, he tells himself, *or grouse*. Ben tries to get out of the way, but his leg lets him down and he falls.

The chairman fires the rifle. The bullet splinters a palm trunk. There is an ominous creaking noise. It grows, accompanied by a great rustling.

'You can't build the world by yourselves, so you come to us and whine when it doesn't turn out how you wanted,' the Chairman continues. 'You're shocked because people want to make money from your ideas. You half-heartedly try to stop them, picketing the headquarters of McDonald's or Coca Cola. You forget that the world prefers standardisation and dull efficiency. It's what your average, telly-ogling proles crave most of all, something boring that does the job and never changes, and they're prepared to give up most of their rights to get it.'

Ben and Miranda are frozen on the spot. Ben looks up and sees that Meera is still reaching for the key.

Dr Samphire follows his eyeline and aims the rifle at the girl on the roof. He wishes he'd brought his glasses with him. He fires. Meera falls in an explosion of glass and with a cry of: 'Jesus Bollocks Son Of A Bitch, not again!'

Ben and Miranda pull Meera from fake ferns and polystyrene-ball earth. As Dr Samphire takes aim once more, he is joined by Fitch and Half-Swan. What a trio they make.

'It always comes down to this,' he tells them. 'Management versus the workforce. Compared with the next generation of wage-slaves, we're radical socialists.' Dr Samphire splits the palm trunk again with his rifle shot. He fires at his staff as they break through into the undergrowth.

Management picks its targets. Fitch attacks Miranda. Half-Swan goes for Ben. Dr Samphire goes after Meera.

Ben's had enough of his half-supervisor. 'Let's see what you're made of,' he suggests, thrusting his hand up inside Half-Swan and pulling down hard. Swan screams, and Ben swings him around, knocking his brains out on a painted concrete tree trunk.

Ben feels better. Killing someone seems to have cleared his head. 'Anybody else want a piece?' he asks, over-confidently.

Miranda tackles Fitch, slamming her to the ground. 'You know,' she tells her, 'we could have been friends if you hadn't tried so hard to be one of the boys.' She slugs her as you would a man, a one-two shot, first one hard in the stomach then a haymaker to the chin, sending her flying off into the bushes and out for the count. 'I saw that in a Tarantino film,' she explains proudly.

Dr Samphire comes after Meera, and gets a clear shot. Meera

is against a wall – there's nowhere left to run.

The Chairman points accusingly. 'You – you're the worst. When we had an Empire, we *owned* people like you. And this – *this* – is the thanks we get.'

He goes to fire, but Meera is free to unleash her formidable martial skills, fairly flying at him with her feet and catching him under the chin. Dr Samphire is fast, though. He has the rifle back in his cradled arm in seconds. Ben knows the Chairman can take them out. He has to do something drastic.

Ben steps forward and raises a placating hand, as Miranda shouts at him.

'This is what I wanted, Miranda,' he says. 'I told you that, the first day. I'm with you, Dr Samphire. Let me help you, and together we can get SymaxCorp back on track.' He walks over to Dr Samphire's side and takes a stand against Miranda and Meera. They can't believe what they're seeing.

The Chairman loves moments like this in the business world. It makes him proud to have been an advisor to both Mrs Thatcher and Mr Blair. 'You chose the victorious side, son. Most sensible. It proves that even someone like you can become a captain of industry.'

As soon as he is close enough, Ben reaches over and grabs the barrel of Dr Samphire's rifle.

The weapon goes off, skimming Ben's arm to plant a third split in the fake palm behind him.

As Ben drops, the great tree comes down. It was never meant to withstand gunfire. As it falls, its concrete sections break apart. The top piece lands squarely on Dr Samphire's head, pulverising his skull into a skillet of bone, pounding him into the ground.

Miranda runs to Ben's side as the deranged Bedlamites, no longer held back by the stand-off, pour into the atrium.

'Fucking arseholes.' Meera has taken to swearing a lot lately. 'Time to go. Did Howard say whether or not the cable tunnel connected to the outside?'

Meera locates the recycling door to the outside world and finds that it's not welded shut after all. Perhaps that was just another lie they fed Howard. Exhausted, they drag themselves inside the tunnel.

Meera checks her watch as they are chased through the claustrophobic tunnel, the mob grabbing and clawing at them. Almost five, nearly time to go home, she can't help thinking. She's always been a city girl.

They emerge, bloodied, burned, scarred, half-naked, in the light of a blazing, blood-red sunset. The rain has stopped. They look back to see the white-eyed staff falling back from the bright tunnel exit like roaches.

'I don't think they want to breathe normal air any longer,' says Meera. 'The doctored stuff is addictive, after all. They'll have to stay inside.'

Behind them, above them, crazed workers hammer silently on the building windows. Something flares and explodes deep inside – but the outside world fails to notice. The tower has become a permanent monument to synaptic disorder, horror, misery, chaos. Perhaps, on a lesser scale, it always was.

'I think maybe it's time to give up my desk job,' says Meera.

Miranda wipes her face. 'Yeah, this won't look too good on your CV.'

They are walking away, they are free, they are safe ... until the tunnel exit bursts open behind them, and a hundred desperate hands claw out. Somehow – they don't know how it happens, it's something that will haunt them forever – some of the hands seize Ben's jacket, and he is hauled back inside. Ben fights furiously as the tunnel shadows swallow him, until he can fight no more. He allows himself to be carried back, all the way into the building's dark heart.

Miranda's screams frighten seagulls above the river.

Meera is forced to pull her away from the outer wall. Around them, home-going commuters move in a solid river, barely pausing to give them notice.

A passing drone complains on his mobile: 'I'm going to have to cancel. I just had a really tough day at work.' Meera shoots him a look. She finds herself still holding Ben's tie. Sadly, she drops it into a nearby litter bin.

Miranda is crying hard. 'Poor Ben,' she says, 'it was the thing he most wanted.' She doesn't seem able to stop the ragged sobs. 'He wanted to be like everyone else in the city.'

The limping, wounded pair gradually merge with the flow of people.

FIVE MONTHS LATER

In the smart, white corporate office, the board meeting comes to an end.

One of the US executives is wrapping up his presentation. 'Due to the unfortunate circumstances surrounding the closure of our London office,' he announces, 'worldwide operations will now be based here in Chicago. The investigation has revealed much that we can learn from past mistakes, and we are completely satisfied that it's impossible for such a problem to arise again. Additionally, I am pleased to announce that SymaxCorp Environment Systems has been awarded the chance to pitch for contracts across all US government buildings.' The office rings to the sound of polite applause.

ONE YEAR AND THREE MONTHS LATER

In the Oval Office of the White House, the President pores over papers on his desk. Above him, tiny air vents open, and there's a gentle, almost comforting hiss. The new unit above his head has a steel label on the edge of the grille. It reads: SYMAXCORP USA.

The President likes it when the fresh air starts up. He always seems to get so much more done. Humming softly to himself, he turns his attention back to the plans for North Korea.

About The Author

Christopher Fowler lives and works in central London, where he is a director of film & design company *Creative Partnership*.

After writing several humour books, including *How To Impersonate Famous People*, he shifted into 'Dark Urban' writing. His first short story anthology *City Jitters* featured interlinked tales of urban malevolence. He has since had eight further volumes of short stories published; *City Jitters Two, The Bureau Of Lost Souls, Sharper Knives, Flesh Wounds, Personal Demons, Uncut, The Devil In Me* and *Demonized*.

His story *The Master Builder* became a movie starring Tippi Hedren and Richard Dean Anderson. Seven other short stories have been filmed as short films, and almost all of his novels are currently under option as features for a wide variety of actors and directors.

The film version of *Left Hand Drive* won Best British Short Film of 1993. *Wageslaves* won the 1998 BFS Best Short Story Of The Year. *On Edge* was a theatrically released short starring Doug 'Pinhead' Bradley and Charley Boorman. Other stories have been published in *Time Out, The Big Issue,* the *Independent On Sunday* and the *Mail On Sunday*.

Christopher reviews for the *Independent on Sunday*, and produces articles for publications including *The Third Alternative, Dazed & Confused* and *Pure* magazine. Recent short stories have appeared in *The Time Out Book Of London Short Stories 2, The New English Library Book Of Internet Stories, Dark Terrors 5 & 6, Best New Horror, London Noir, Neon Lit., A Book Of Two Halves, Vengeance Is, Love In Vein 2, Year's Best Fantasy & Horror, Destination Unknown, 100 Fiendish Little Frightmares, The Time Out Book Of New York Stories* and many others.

Other Telos Titles Available

TIME HUNTER

A range of high-quality, original paperback novellas featuring the adventures in time of Honoré Lechasseur. Part mystery, part detective story, part dark fantasy, part science fiction ... these books are guaranteed to enthral fans of good fiction everywhere, and are in the spirit of our acclaimed range of *Doctor Who* Novellas.

THE WINNING SIDE by LANCE PARKIN
Emily is dead! Killed by an unknown assailant. Honoré and Emily find themselves caught up in a plot reaching from the future to their past, and with their very existence, not to mention the future of the entire world, at stake, can they unravel the mystery before it is too late?
An adventure in time and space.
£7.99 (+ £1.50 UK p&p) Standard p/b ISBN 1-903889-35-9 (pb)
£25.00 (+ £1.50 UK p&p) Deluxe h/b ISBN 1-903889-36-7 (hb)

THE TUNNEL AT THE END OF THE LIGHT by STEFAN PETRUCHA
In the heart of post-war London, a bomb is discovered lodged at a disused station between Green Park and Hyde Park Corner. The bomb detonates, and as the dust clears, it becomes apparent that *something* has been awakened. Strange half-human creatures attack the workers at the site, hungrily searching for anything containing sugar ...
Meanwhile, Honoré and Emily are contacted by eccentric poet Randolph Crest, who believes himself to be the target of these subterranean creatures. The ensuing investigation brings Honoré and Emily up against a terrifying force from deep beneath the

earth, and one which even with their combined powers, they may have trouble stopping.

An adventure in time and space.

£7.99 (+ £1.50 UK p&p) Standard p/b ISBN 1-903889-37-5 (pb)
£25.00 (+ £1.50 UK p&p) Deluxe h/b ISBN 1-903889-38-3 (hb)

THE CLOCKWORK WOMAN by CLAIRE BOTT

Honoré and Emily find themselves imprisoned in the 19th Century by a celebrated inventor ... but help comes from an unexpected source – a humanoid automaton created by and to give pleasure to its owner. As the trio escape to London, they are unprepared for what awaits them, and at every turn it seems impossible to avert what fate may have in store for the Clockwork Woman.

An adventure in time and space.

£7.99 (+ £1.50 UK p&p) Standard p/b ISBN 1-903889-39-1 (pb)
£25.00 (+ £1.50 UK p&p) Deluxe h/b ISBN 1-903889-40-5 (hb)

HORROR/FANTASY

URBAN GOTHIC: LACUNA & OTHER TRIPS ed. DAVID J. HOWE
Stories by Graham Masterton, Christopher Fowler, Simon Clark, Debbie Bennett, Paul Finch, Steve Lockley & Paul Lewis.
Based on the Channel 5 horror series.
SOLD OUT

THE MANITOU by GRAHAM MASTERTON
A 25th Anniversary author's preferred edition of this classic horror novel. An ancient Red Indian medicine man is reincarnated in modern day New York intent on reclaiming his land from the white men.
£9.99 (+ £2.50 UK p&p) Standard p/b ISBN: 1-903889-70-7
£30.00 (+ £2.50 UK p&p) Deluxe h/b ISBN: 1-903889-71-5

CAPE WRATH by PAUL FINCH
Death and horror on a deserted Scottish island as an ancient Viking warrior chief returns to life.
£8.00 (+ £1.50 UK p&p) Standard p/b ISBN: 1-903889-60-X

KING OF ALL THE DEAD by STEVE LOCKLEY & PAUL LEWIS
The king of all the dead will have what is his.
£8.00 (+ £1.50 UK p&p) Standard p/b ISBN: 1-903889-61-8

GUARDIAN ANGEL by STEPHANIE BEDWELL-GRIME
Devilish fun as Guardian Angel Porsche Winter loses a soul to the devil …
£9.99 (+ £2.50 UK p&p) Standard p/b ISBN: 1-903889-62-6

ASPECTS OF A PSYCHOPATH by ALISTAIR LANGSTON
Goes deeper than ever before into the twisted psyche of a serial killer. Horrific, graphic and gripping, this book is not for the

squeamish.

£8.00 (+ £1.50 UK p&p) Standard p/b ISBN: 1-903889-63-4

SPECTRE by STEPHEN LAWS

The inseparable Byker Chapter: six boys, one girl, growing up together in the back streets of Newcastle. Now memories are all that Richard Eden has left, and one treasured photograph. But suddenly, inexplicably, the images of his companions start to fade, and as they vanish, so his friends are found dead and mutilated. Something is stalking the Chapter, picking them off one by one, something connected with their past, and with the girl they used to know.

£9.99 (+ £2.50 UK p&p) Standard p/b ISBN: 1-903889-72-3

TV/FILM GUIDES

BEYOND THE GATE: THE UNOFFICIAL AND UNAUTHORISED GUIDE TO STARGATE SG-1 by KEITH TOPPING
Complete episode guide to the middle of Season 6 (episode 121) of the popular TV show.
£9.99 (+ £2.50 UK p&p) Standard p/b ISBN: 1-903889-50-2

A DAY IN THE LIFE: THE UNOFFICIAL AND UNAUTHORISED GUIDE TO 24 by KEITH TOPPING
Complete episode guide to the first season of the popular TV show.
£9.99 (+ £2.50 p&p) Standard p/b ISBN: 1-903889-53-7

THE TELEVISION COMPANION: THE UNOFFICIAL AND UNAUTHORISED GUIDE TO DOCTOR WHO by DAVID J HOWE & STEPHEN JAMES WALKER
Complete episode guide to the popular TV show.
£14.99 (+ £4.75 UK p&p) Standard p/b ISBN: 1-903889-51-0

LIBERATION: THE UNOFFICIAL AND UNAUTHORISED GUIDE TO BLAKE'S 7 by ALAN STEVENS & FIONA MOORE
Complete episode guide to the popular TV show.
Featuring a foreword by David Maloney
£9.99 (+ £2.50 UK p&p) Standard p/b ISBN: 1-903889-54-5

HOWE'S TRANSCENDENTAL TOYBOX: SECOND EDITION by DAVID J HOWE & ARNOLD T BLUMBERG
Complete guide to Doctor Who Merchandise.
£25.00 (+ £4.75 UK p&p) Standard p/b ISBN: 1-903889-56-1

HANK JANSON

Classic pulp crime thrillers from the 1940s and 1950s.

TORMENT by HANK JANSON £9.99 (+ £1.50 UK p&p) Standard p/b ISBN: 1-903889-80-4
WOMEN HATE TILL DEATH by HANK JANSON £9.99 (+ £1.50 UK p&p) Standard p/b ISBN: 1-903889-81-2
SOME LOOK BETTER DEAD by HANK JANSON £9.99 (+ £1.50 UK p&p) Standard p/b ISBN: 1-903889-82-0
SKIRTS BRING ME SORROW by HANK JANSON £9.99 (+ £1.50 UK p&p) Standard p/b ISBN: 1-903889-83-9
WHEN DAMES GET TOUGH by HANK JANSON £9.99 (+ £1.50 UK p&p) Standard p/b ISBN: 1-903889-85-5

THE TRIALS OF HANK JANSON by STEVE HOLLAND
Biography of Stephen D Frances, the writer of the Hank Janson books.
£12.99 (+ £2.50 UK p&p) Standard p/b ISBN: 1-903889-84-7

The prices shown are correct at time of going to press. However, the publishers reserve the right to increase prices from those previously advertised without prior notice.

TELOS PUBLISHING
c/o Beech House, Chapel Lane, Moulton, Cheshire, CW9 8PQ,
England
Email: orders@telos.co.uk
Web: www.telos.co.uk

To order copies of any Telos books, please visit our website where there are full details of all titles and facilities for worldwide credit card online ordering, or send a cheque or postal order (UK only) for the appropriate amount (including postage and packing), together with details of the book(s) you require, plus your name and address to the above address. Overseas readers please send two international reply coupons for details of prices and postage rates.